THE MERCENARY

Order of the Broken Blade

CECELIA MECCA

Altiora Press

To my readers, always.

needed in this particular case. He knew the man personally and was sure of his leanings. Perhaps Guy should have allowed Conrad to be the one to speak to the bishop. But somehow, as it always had been with these vague notions of his, Guy knew this task was meant for him.

He took a deep breath.

"We've formed an order. Our aim is to amass enough support that we may compel the king to adjust his policies."

He had the man's attention now.

"He will never agree to do such a thing," the bishop said, his voice flat.

The bishop had good reason to be skeptical. Had the king been an agreeable man, predisposed to listen to his people, there would have been no need for the order. But King John's demands were outrageous, his tax increases so high some barons had been forced to forfeit their properties rather than pay the money they owed.

"He will agree or see himself at war with his barons," Guy boldly claimed.

If Bishop Salerno had looked surprised earlier, he seemed even more so now.

Dammit Conrad, you better be right.

"Your plan? And the men in your order?" His mask of indifference back in place, the bishop folded his hands on his lap, the glint of a particularly massive gold ring drawing Guy's eye.

Once he uttered the names, there would be no turning back. There was already no turning back.

"Conrad Saint-Clair, the Earl of Licheford. Terric Kennaugh, chief of Clan Kennaugh and Earl of Dromsley," he said, naming the Scot's two titles. "And Sir Lancelin Wayland of Marwood and now lord of Tuleen."

Guy shrugged internally. He was nothing if not honest.

The bishop extended his hand, and Guy sat, as indicated, in front of the fire. Though he'd been in the man's presence all evening, he had little indication of the man's temperament. He knew only what Conrad, their leader, had told him. That Bishop Salerno supported the order's cause. Like them, he was alarmed by King John's overreach. In truth, nothing else mattered.

When the abbess closed the door, Guy waited until he was sure she had left and was out of hearing. He tried not to stare at the rings bedecking every finger of the old man's hands. Such wealth could serve a better purpose, but saying so, or even acting like he thought so, would not win him any friends.

"So you count the Earl of Licheford a friend?" the bishop asked him.

Guy pretended not to notice the bishop's uneasiness around him. He was a mercenary, not a murderer. Although some may question the distinction.

"Conrad is more than a friend."

Aware his next statement could see him executed as a traitor if said to the wrong person, Guy put his faith in Conrad and Terric's insistence that Bishop Salerno would indeed support their cause.

"He is an ally in our quest for King John to answer for his actions."

For the first time that evening, the bishop's stoicism was replaced with surprise.

"And how," he said carefully, "do you propose to accomplish such a thing?"

The bishop's intelligent eyes looked through him as he awaited an answer. The others they'd brought to their cause over the last few months had required more delicacy. But Conrad had assured him none was

"You may use the calefactory, if you please," the abbess said to Bishop Salerno after they finished their meager meal. "I will see you are not disturbed." She didn't spare a glance for Guy, although that didn't surprise him. He could tell she was leery of him, and his purpose here.

Smart woman.

Guy followed the bishop into the room. Three nuns stood at the fire, their hands outstretched, although they quickstepped away from the hearth when they spotted the visitors. They nodded to the bishop in deference as they passed, ignoring Guy.

With luck, this would be the first and only night he'd spend at the cold and unwelcoming Holybourne Abbey. When Guy had spoken of his mission with the rest of the Order of the Broken Blade, his friend Terric had burst into laughter. So many women, none of whom would fall at his feet the moment Guy stepped into the room. He'd laughed at the time, but in truth, it was slightly disconcerting. He was unused to receiving so little attention from the fairer sex.

And he liked it not at all.

That he should admit the fact, even to himself . . .

admonished both of them for their forwardness. But he'd have done it with a smile on his face.

Sabine pushed aside the thought.

A handsome knight. Friend to the bishop.

She really should eat her soup and make her way to the kitchen, where she'd be expected to work until vespers. It would be best to forget about a man who was as likely to tell the Reverend Mother on her as he was to help her escape.

But once the thought took hold, she could not put it aside so easily.

words as she had since coming here. Her parents would be both surprised and appalled at the woman she'd become.

"I understand."

Sister Christine did let go of her then, but she continued to glare at her as if Sabine had breathed a word of dissent. Turning slowly so as not to anger her further, Sabine held her head high and walked the length of the cloister to the hall. Nuns sat side by side in rows, mostly silent other than a few whispered words. Moments after she sat, another novice plopped down a bowl of soup in front of her. Sabine had served both the morning and midday meal, but still the young woman glared at her as if she'd shirked her duties.

Unlike Sabine, she wanted to be here. Had chosen to become a nun and devote her life to God. So why the dour disposition?

"He seems to know the bishop," said the older nun beside her.

"Who?" she asked, attempting to peer over the tables that separated them from their august visitor.

"We've another visitor this eve."

"A knight," whispered the nun to her left.

Sabine couldn't remember her name, but she liked this one. She had an easy way about her, and when she smiled, it was obvious she meant it. The smile she was giving Sabine now looked almost . . . conspiratorial, as if their new visitor was . . .

"Is he handsome?"

A certain sparkle in the nun's eyes was her answer. The nun seated directly across from Sabine gave her a stern glance that cautioned her not to say such things.

It was the kind of remark she may have made to her mother. Who would have laughed as her father these past three days, preferring to eat in her small chamber. Such an arrangement robbed Sister Christine of the chance to "better" her, however, and the sister often sought her out.

"Your presence is required at the evening meal."

"Reverend Mother gave me leave," she whispered in her most reverent tone. One she'd perfected of late.

The nun, her headpiece hiding all but her pale face riddled with wrinkles, was apparently not pleased with that particular response. Her eyes pinned Sabine to the spot. "Bishop Salerno is in residence," she said, her tone brooking no argument. "You will take your meal in the refectory."

Eyes downcast Sabine moved to make her way through the cloister to do just that when the nun's hand wrapped around her wrist.

"And you will quit your attempts at escape. Many would be grateful for the opportunity you've been given."

Her hand squeezed.

"Reverend Mother has been too tolerant."

Sabine did not attempt to disengage her hand. Nor did she question the nun or comment on what she had left out of her speech. All knew the abbess was ill, even though she went about her duties as if well. Sabine had only been at the abbey one month, and even she could discern a difference in the elderly woman's health. Sister Christine clearly had ambitions, and once she took control of the abbey, she would not be so tolerant.

"Aye, Sister. If you will pardon me?"

She attempted to pull her hand away, to no avail.

"You will be a Bride of Christ, child. Your haughtiness is not welcome here."

Haughtiness? Sabine had never been accused of such in her life. But then, she'd never said so few

CHAPTER 1

S t. *Andrew Holybourne Abbey, England, 1214*
Lady Sabine never wanted to be a nun.

She'd attempted to escape the abbey twice. On her last attempt, the monk with whom she'd arranged to leave had fallen ill and later died, a horrible omen, if one believed in such things. The time before that, she'd gone off alone, only to be spied by a stable boy, who had promptly told the abbess. Sabine had been given a warning—one more attempt and Lord Burge would be notified of her antics.

She shuddered at the thought.

"There you are," said a familiar voice, the tone thick with accusation.

Sister Christine, the very woman she'd snuck out of the sext to avoid. The bishop was visiting, which had driven the sister into a frenzy. She had never taken to Sabine and had begun to critique her every action, especially at mealtimes. "Straighten your shoulders" or "Do not eat with such force" were admonishments she had heard for the past three days at nearly every meal.

How does one eat with force, precisely? Sabine wanted to ask but knew doing so would only anger Sister Christine. And so she had taken to avoiding meals

CHAPTER 3

A t the sound of the wooden chairs scraping against the floor, Sabine moved away, flattening her back against the cold stone wall. She swallowed. Hard. The plan that had formed in her head was surely the height of folly, and yet . . .

Seize opportunities that lay themselves at your feet, Sabine.

Hadn't her parents taught her that? When the door finally opened, she envisioned Sister Christine's frown of displeasure and took a deep, steadying breath. She had a way out, finally, and she would use it. She had to.

"I bid you a good eve, sir," the bishop said as he walked through the door.

He stopped, seeing her, but Sabine was not looking at the bishop. Instead, she focused on the man who'd just exited behind him. They both turned her way, and courtesy of the wall torch mounted next to them, she could see the traitor clearly.

She couldn't do it.

Too handsome by far, he stared straight at her. She knew she should shift her gaze, but she'd never followed the rules of the nunnery, despite Christine's warnings. And she simply could not do so now.

The more she looked at him, the more certain she was this was not the man for her. He could not be controlled, which made him quite incompatible for her purposes.

The two men walked by her, the bishop murmuring his thanks for protecting their privacy. She had indeed been sent for that purpose, although the nun who'd given her the duty certainly hadn't known what she would witness. Sabine did look down then, but not in reverence.

"'Twas my pleasure," she whispered as the men walked by her.

Sandalwood.

The traitor smelled like sandalwood.

She continued to stare at her feet as they moved away, chiding herself for a fool's plan. Sabine knew nothing of the visitor. Well, very little.

She knew he plotted against the king, boldly risking his life to garner the bishop's support. Unless, of course, he knew the man's leanings, which, as she thought about it, was a likely scenario.

She also knew he was fiercely loyal, willing to give his life for the others with whom he plotted.

Sabine could sense the danger in him as well.

"You want something of me." The voice was husky and deep, a bit wild.

Her head whipped up. He stood inches away from her, his presence engulfing her. How had she not heard him returning?

Sabine glanced down the corridor.

"Gone to bed," he said of the bishop.

Sabine had not expected this conversation. Not after she'd rejected her hasty plan to use what she'd heard.

"I want nothing from you, sir."

His eyes were brown. But like hers, they held many different shades.

"Liar."

She gasped. What manner of man was he to say such a thing? To a nun. A stranger.

The kind of man who would rebel against his king.

When he took a step toward her, Sabine did not shrink away. Not that she could move very far with her back up against the wall.

"Kind of you to guard our conversation, Sister."

She'd not correct him. Nor would she answer him, as he was clearly suspicious of her. Did he correctly surmise that she had heard the very dangerous words he'd spoken to Bishop Salerno?

She watched him carefully, looking for any sign that her original plan might be feasible after all.

"A woman of few words."

There was no mistaking his meaning. Before her parents' death, many men had come to Cottingham to seek her hand in marriage. More than one of them had spoken to her in just such a tone, though none had been quite so handsome.

But that he flirted with a woman he believed to be a nun told Sabine all she needed to know. Aye, she desperately wanted to leave Holybourne.

But not with him.

"I've nothing to say," she lied. Sabine might have said quite a bit if he'd been more approachable.

"Your eyes tell a different tale."

She sucked in a deep breath.

He smiled then. Slow, taunting. As if he were privy to a secret he'd never tell.

"They move about more quickly than they should. And you closed them a moment ago. Briefly but long enough to signify deep thought."

It took her a moment to understand.

He spoke of her eyes. He was telling her how he knew she lied.

Sabine congratulated herself on her very accurate

assessment of this man. Dangerous and cunning. Her father would have quite liked him.

He moved so quickly, Sabine hardly had time to react. If any other man had grabbed her wrist that way, she'd have done exactly what her father had taught her. And he would be bowled over just now, clutching his private area.

But she found she wanted to see what he had to say.

Firmly escorting her into the room he'd just left, this time shutting the door completely, he let go of her wrist and pinned her to the spot with his stare.

"Talk to me," he said, his tone harder than it had been earlier. "Now."

CHAPTER 4

Bloody hell.

Guy had bedded all sorts of women. But never a nun. The thought of it sickened him even as his cock grew hard looking at her. He couldn't see her hair, but Guy could easily imagine it. In his mind, it was a glossy chestnut brown.

Her temper only made her more desirable. Although he had never once noticed a woman's nose before, hers, like every other feature on her face, displayed her anger. Her nostrils flared, as indignant as the look in her light eyes, which had not chosen just one color. That mesmerizing collection of brown and green and blue pinned him to the spot.

Knowing he should back away but unable to do so, Guy simply stared back, waiting for an answer. Looking at her in a way no man should look at a nun.

"I must get back," she said at last. "Sister Christine will be looking for me."

"Sister Christine is a whey-faced prig."

His nun gasped. And then covered her mouth with her hand. Guy supposed he should have tempered his honest response. Until he realized she was smiling. Nay, laughing. Small lines crinkled around her eyes as they danced with merriment. He'd thought her beautiful before, but he amended his opinion.

She was perfection.

"So you don't care for her either?"

She shook her head, still laughing. "Pardon me. 'Tis unkind of me to laugh at such an insult."

"'Tis unkind of her to treat others as she does."

Guy had met her only once, but it was enough for him to take her measure. He was about to ask again if his nun had something to tell him when she suddenly stopped laughing. Her laughing eyes had been replaced by such a fierce expression of determination, he was momentarily taken aback.

"Take me with you."

Surely she did not just say that.

It was his turn to laugh.

"This place must be affecting me more than I feared. It sounded as if you said—"

"I've no wish to be here and want you to take me with you."

"You've no wish . . ." This conversation was not progressing as he'd expected. "Sister?" He didn't even know her name.

"Sabine."

"Sister Sabine. I cannot simply abscond from Holybourne with one of its nuns."

"You can and you will."

She was serious.

The woman really wanted him to take her away from the abbey. He had so many questions, but none mattered. Such a thing was not possible.

"You cannot come with me. Aside from the fact that it is simply not done, even if I wanted to take you," he stammered, "I could not do so."

"Because of your mission?"

His eyes narrowed.

"I know of your plot. And of Bishop Salerno's role

in it. And because I heard every word spoken in here, you *will* take me with you."

Gone was the mild-mannered nun he'd passed in the corridor. She looked at him with eyes blazing with conviction.

"You think to . . . blackmail me?"

"Call it what you will."

"Then I'll call it as I see it. And I will not be blackmailed. By a nun."

She appeared too unconcerned by his statement for his comfort.

He would play along.

"Why, pray tell, do you wish to leave Holybourne? And why do you wish to do so with me?"

She frowned as if the question were too bothersome to contemplate.

"I stay here against my will. The fact that I need you, or anyone, to escape is more vexing to me than you know, sir. But I do, and I'll continue to need protection once I leave. For a time. I am the ward of Lord Burge, who installed me here for coin. The abbess, of course, will retrieve the money from him should my escape attempt prove fruitful."

By God's own nails, this woman was actually requesting his assistance for her escape.

"And how, if I may be so bold to ask, am I to offer such protection? If our escape attempt were successful?"

Guy wasn't even sure why he asked such a question. Because it would not be happening.

She lifted her chin, giving him the distinct impression he wouldn't like what she had to say next.

"As my husband, of course."

CHAPTER 5

She hadn't meant to say it quite that way. But Sister Christine really would be looking for her. The poor woman she'd convinced to switch duties with her would likely not remain quiet for long. Which meant she didn't have time to bandy about.

"What is your name?" she asked.

"My . . ." He did take a step back from her then. "A fine time to ask such a question. After that outrageous proposal?"

"This?" She indicated her habit. "I am no nun."

His eyes widened. "A novice, then?"

"Nay. Oblate. And very much against my will."

"You . . . are not a nun."

Had she not just said as much? "Nay. But I am in need of a husband."

Sabine would have laughed at his expression were the situation not so serious.

"I am the ward of Lord Burge, who was overlord to my father, Robert de Stuteville, lord of Cottingham. When he was killed . . ." She paused, leaving much of the story out. "Lord Burge decided three unwed daughters, and three dowries, were too many for him. Having no desire to produce a fourth dowry, he sold me instead to Holybourne."

"It seems you're more in need of a rescue than a husband, my lady." He seemed inclined to offer her neither.

"I hoped you could provide both," she said. "As well as your name."

"Perhaps you should inquire the name of your potential husband before proposing marriage?" he said, his tone and demeanor more accusatory than his words suggested.

"I asked, if you will recall."

"I don't typically offer it to people attempting to persuade me at pain of retribution."

No doubt Sister Christine had noted her absence already. She was running out of time.

"I am sorry for such directness," she said, not sorry at all. "But we really should be leaving immediately. This night, if it pleases you."

He laughed then, tossing his head back with abandon.

The man really was quite handsome, especially when he smiled. Or at least he would be, to a woman who liked danger.

She did not.

"I," he emphasized, "will be leaving on the morrow. Alone."

Sabine shook her head. "If you do so, all will know of your plans. Namely, to send the French mercenaries King John hired back to France." She ignored the fact that his gaze turned murderous. "As a part of a rebellion against our sovereign."

"You were sent to listen to a very private conversation."

"Nay. I was sent to ensure it remained private. That Reverend Mother did not fully close the door was a happy circumstance." She paused, then added, "I can offer coin as well."

Silently thanking her mother for not having

trusted Lord Burge as her father did, she waited for this stranger to decide on the course of her future.

"I've no need of a wife."

He attempted to walk past her then.

Was he really leaving? She couldn't let him!

"But your plot," she said, desperate. "The king."

He stopped, but only momentarily.

"I will not be blackmailed. By anyone." His tone was harsh, accusatory. As it should be.

Sabine clarified to his back. "I do not wish to remain married. I only suggest it because I will remain Burge's ward unless I marry. He will not be happy when the abbess demands the return of her coin, and he *will* find me."

He reached for the door.

She had nothing left to offer. Sabine hated herself for her desperation, but she simply could not remain here. And an opportunity such as this one would not present itself again. Not before she would be forced to say the vows that would bind her to this abbey forever.

Placing her hand atop his, she offered all she had left to give.

"Please."

Sabine hated him in that moment. Hated that his refusal had left her no other choice. His hand quickly covered hers. Spinning her around, he pinned her to the very door he'd nearly just opened.

"Let us be clear"—he grasped her wrists and held them on either side of her, and Sabine gasped as he took the final step that closed the small gap between them—"about what you're now offering."

Her heart raced as the foolishness of her actions finally penetrated. She'd threatened a man who'd committed treason. Goaded him and then suggested he take the coin she would need if she were to survive. And then she'd touched him and said "please," silently offering much, much more.

But what choice did she have?

"I take you from here"—his thumbs dug into her wrists—"and you remain silent. We marry to dissuade Lord Burge from pursuit . . . and then become man and wife in truth."

Nay, not digging, precisely. More like circling.

She swallowed. And nodded.

"When your guardian stops his pursuit, we part ways. Do I have the right of it?"

Sabine nodded again, not daring to speak.

"Divorce is costly, my lady. As I'm sure you know."

"I have coin," she reminded him.

As abruptly as he'd grabbed her, her would-be husband let go. Her chest rose and fell, the fireplace hissing in its insistence on being heard over the beating of her heart.

She really should be afraid of him. Of how he looked at her just now. But she wasn't. Maybe her desperation made it so—she really did want to leave this place—or maybe she trusted her instincts more than the proper part of her that insisted she ought to run far away from him. Forget this entire plan.

"Guy Lavallis of Cradney Wrens."

She blinked.

"You should know your husband's name."

CHAPTER 6

O ne day, your hasty actions will turn on you with a
vengeance.
       Terric had said as much to him when last
they spoke, just before this trip to Holybourne. Upon
reflection, Aceline, whom Guy had once fought beside as a member of Bande de Valeur, had said much
the same.

It would seem both men had taken his measure.

As he waited in their predetermined spot near the
abbey's stables, Guy refused to doubt himself. He'd
seen such sentiments get men killed. But that didn't
mean he was happy about the prospect of marrying a
stranger, or any woman really. Even one as beautiful
as Lady Sabine.

Not Sister Sabine.

I am no nun.

No four words had ever jolted him as those had,
the effects of which he still carried with him. Bloody
hell, the lady had blackmailed him, yet all he could
think of was tearing off that headpiece to see more
than just her face.

A noise from within demanded his attention.
When a stable boy walked past a moment later, Guy
stepped deeper into the shadows. It had gone against

his instincts to leave Sabine alone with information that could destroy his mission. But her obvious desperation to leave the abbey had inspired him to do something quite unusual.

He trusted her. If only to gather her belongings to meet him here.

After speaking to the bishop again, explaining that he would be leaving sooner than anticipated, Guy had decided against seeking out the Reverend Mother. She would know in the morn he was responsible for Lady Sabine's hasty departure. A pretty farewell, under the circumstances, seemed ill-advised.

He'd come for Bishop Salerno's support and received it. Nothing else mattered. Except keeping his companion quiet long enough to ensure she did not jeopardize his mission.

"Are you there?" she called out, barely attempting to whisper.

She would get them both killed.

Guy grabbed her arm before she even saw him. "Shhh."

He nodded toward Arion, his jet-black destrier hidden in the shadows behind the stables. Understanding, she allowed him to lift her into the saddle. He nearly groaned as he did so, his suspicions confirmed.

The long black frock attempted to hide a small waist and curves that begged to be explored. And it mostly succeeded. But he knew better now. And damned if the biggest threat to the order's rebellion wasn't this slip of a woman with dangerous knowledge and an even more dangerous body.

Guy didn't waste time dwelling on thoughts of her waist, or any other part of the non-nun's body. Being caught absconding with a lord's daughter, one the Reverend Mother had paid to acquire, was not part of his plan this eve.

Tying off her bag, Guy mounted in front of Lady Sabine, letting Arion's movement dictate Lady Sabine's actions. When she did indeed wrap her arms around his waist, Guy smiled into the night. He had no use for a wife. But if this woman willingly gave herself to him, Guy would accept the distraction.

One day, your hasty actions will turn on you with a vengeance.

He'd not yet fathered a bastard babe, to his knowledge. And Guy had no intention of doing so with his soon-to-be discarded wife. Thankfully, there were ways around such an affliction.

"I am surprised you took my offer."

He didn't turn in his saddle or acknowledge her words except to nod toward the abbey's lights, which they passed as they rode forward. Silence was their ally, and she seemed to understand his meaning. But as the torches dimmed, Guy's grip on the reins relaxed. The gates of St. Andrew Holybourne Abbey were neither closed nor guarded. As they slowly passed through marshland in the darkness, quiet pervaded all around them.

"Your offer was quite compelling," he said at last.

"Not to share your treasonous plan?" She said the word with less vehemence than he'd expected.

"Nay."

Guy let her think on that answer as he smoothed his mount's mane. Arion did well at night, his steps sure. But a bit of encouragement never hurt matters.

He could tell the moment she understood. Her arms stiffened against him, and Lady Sabine shifted in the saddle. Cursing under his breath, Guy concentrated on the black fabric of her skirts, which hung across his leg.

Think of her as you first saw her. As a nun.

It didn't work.

So instead, as they rode farther away from the

abbey, he did something even more unusual than agreeing to take a bride.

Guy talked to her.

Not that he didn't enjoy talking to women. Before they fell into his bed.

"So why do you believe this Lord Burge will attempt to reclaim you? Surely if we make our way to Noreham Castle, he will not follow." Noreham was where he'd find Bande de Valeur—the next part of his mission.

If the lady had overheard his entire conversation with the bishop, she already knew their destination. There was no reason to disguise it.

"You underestimate him, *sir*."

The soft-spoken nun was all but gone. His companion had an acid tongue, apparently, and was not afraid to use it.

"Guy. 'Tis unseemly to speak so formally to a man who will be your husband."

For some reason, Guy wished to goad her.

"Unseemly?"

He smiled into the night. Oh, it was almost too easy to set her off.

"More so than the current situation which I find myself in?"

"When I claim my payment for services rendered, I'd very much enjoy hearing my name from your lips. My given name, that is."

Her sound of disgust, not unexpected, was followed by silence.

"How could I have thought you honorable?" she muttered. Prompting him to laugh, too loudly.

"I assure you"—he braced himself for a tongue-lashing—"Sabine. I am many things, but no one has ever accused me of being honorable."

He'd thought she'd respond to that, if only to lambaste him for using her name without permission, but she merely sniffed.

"Will we travel all night?" she asked some time later.

It was only then Guy realized she was likely unused to riding long distances. A damned inconvenience.

"Aye," he said, ignoring her wiggling in the saddle.

When she failed to voice a complaint, he reluctantly added, "We should arrive at St. Mary's-upon-Kingsgate well before sunrise."

"Another abbey?"

He slowed then, turning to his companion.

"We made a bargain, my lady. And I mean to honor it. A priest resides there, too ill to travel but well enough to perform a quick wedding ceremony."

It struck Guy that they'd stopped moving. He must have given Arion the command to halt without realizing it. Sabine's grip on his waist slacked as he watched her. Her full lips flattened—she understood what he meant, although he couldn't tell how she felt about it.

He may be a cad, but he would never shy from his word, once given. And though he hardly knew this vision in a nun's habit, the very one who'd blackmailed him into their current situation, they would marry that night. He cared little for the idea of her Lord Burge making any claims on her while she remained under his care.

In the meantime . . .

"Wedding ceremony."

"Aye, my lady. 'Twas a condition of your terms, was it not?"

She lifted her chin. "Sabine."

"Pardon?"

"Sabine. If we are to be wed, you should continue to call me by my given name."

laughed. Hard. As heartily as the time Terric Conrad took a dunk in a river they'd been crossing, one pulling the other down as he and Lance watched in amusement. This journey may take longer than he'd anticipated, but it would certainly be more enjoyable for her company.

CHAPTER 7

Who was this man, truly?

Sabine followed him into the second abbey just as the sun began to rise. This one was small, just two buildings and a chapel. And even though they could not possibly know she'd escaped from Holybourne the previous night, her legs felt heavier and heavier with each step toward the small stone building.

When a woman appeared at the door, fully dressed despite the hour, Sabine knew immediately this was the Reverend Mother. Her eyes widened upon seeing Sabine standing behind Guy.

"Apologies for the hour," he began, Guy's tone shockingly sweet, "but will you please send for Father Wheeland? Tell him Guy Lavallis requests his presence in the chapel. We shall meet him there."

With a slight bow, he turned and began to walk toward that very place. Sabine stood stock-still, she and the Reverend Mother staring at each other. Eventually the nun turned without a word back into the building, leaving Sabine to follow Guy toward the darkened chapel.

Nay, not darkened. As they entered, wall torches on either side of the altar lent an eerie glow to the early morning scene. Small, like the rest of St. Mary's, it was nevertheless well-appointed.

Sabine took a seat on the closest bench, weary from riding all night. Her backside screamed in protest even though she sat near the very edge of the seat.

He was watching her, those variegated eyes studying her.

Was she really going to marry this man? A stranger. A mercenary. A traitor to the king?

Aye. The alternative was one she'd been living these past months, and it was unacceptable.

"Reconsidering?"

He strode toward her, sitting on the bench opposite her.

"Nay. Are you?"

He looked as if she'd offended him. "If you are truly in danger of pursuit from Lord Burge while you are in my care, then my mission is in danger of discovery."

She supposed that was a nay.

"Why do you believe this priest will marry us without preparation at such an hour?"

He smiled. Not just any smile, but a knowing one that told her clearly she did not want the answer to that question.

So he had information on this priest. Or something equally nefarious.

"Who are you?"

He didn't hesitate. "Guy Lavallis of Cradney Wrens. Half English and half French, courtesy of my mother. Born and raised a mercenary, like my father. Blackmailed into marriage by a lovely nun who, by the by, is wearing a habit to her own wedding."

Sabine winced. To hear what she'd done in such terms . . .

Nay, she would not apologize. To him. To herself.

She'd done what was needed, and her father had always said that women apologize far too often.

Sabine reached up to remove the headdress. She'd become so accustomed to wearing it, she had completely forgotten it was there.

A voice from behind stopped her.

"What urgent business demands such an early waking for an old man?"

The priest wasn't happy. But he was indeed old. Dressed in a brown robe that looked as if he'd worn it every day for many years, the white-haired man ambled toward them, stopping when Sabine turned to face him.

"Good morn, Father." Guy stood. "If you'll see to the business of my marriage vows, I would be grateful for it."

Sabine nearly burst into laughter at the man's stricken expression. For the rest of her days she would remember the shock on his face.

"You go too far this time, Lavallis. I certainly cannot perform such a deed—"

"She is no nun." Guy frowned. "An oblate. And not of her choosing."

Sabine stood and made her way toward the ancient priest.

"Greetings, Father." Should she share her name? She glanced back at Guy, who nodded to indicate it was indeed safe. Of course, if this man was to marry them, he would certainly need it.

"Lady Sabine de Stuteville. I was indeed an oblate and did not enter the vocation of my own volition."

He did not appear convinced.

"And you take this man," he said none too kindly, "as your husband willingly?"

His tone gave her pause. The priest obviously knew Guy, though their relationship did not seem an overly friendly one.

She wondered briefly what her parents would have thought of this decision. Would they have approved? Certainly Guy was not the type of man they'd have chosen for her husband, but neither would they have wished for her to be trapped inside a nunnery.

Thankfully, this was nothing more than a temporary condition.

"Aye, Father."

Guy was watching her.

As the priest made his way toward the front of the chapel, he continued to look at her as if waiting for her to run screaming from the chapel.

He would be waiting a long time.

When he reached the front, he sighed deeply and waved them both over, indicating where they were to stand. They got into position, and without further preamble, the priest began the proceedings.

Her wedding.

Guy cleared his throat.

The priest stopped and looked at him. Then they both stared at her.

Guy glanced up, toward her head, which was when she realized she'd never taken off her headpiece. Finally understanding the priest's stricken expression, she reached up, untucked the pins that held it so close to her face, and removed the headdress. Turning toward a bench, she placed it there, wishing she could change her gown as well.

Turning back toward the men, Sabine froze at Guy's expression.

Had she done something wrong? His eyes were as wide as two circular trenchers, his lips slightly parted. The roguishly handsome man promptly burst into laughter, as he seemed prone to do.

What had she gotten herself into?

CHAPTER 8

Guy approached his wife's door, still amazed a private chamber had been available at the small abbey. He had slept in the stable loft, a fitful sleep given the circumstances. In the unlikely event they were already being followed, Guy did not wish to linger.

His wife.

Smiling at the thought of telling his friends, none of whom would believe he was a married man, Guy knocked on the door.

No answer.

He imagined Sabine lying in bed, a mass of auburn hair spilling around her pillow. He thought back to the moment she'd finally removed her headpiece that morning. The sight of all that glossy hair, tumbling around her lovely face . . . it had shocked him that such a woman would willingly give herself to him in marriage. Even Father Wheeland could not contain his surprise.

Guy knocked again.

"A moment, if you please."

Oddly, he felt no animosity toward the woman who'd entrapped him into marriage. Neither did he feel as if a noose hung around his neck. For a man

who'd vowed never to marry, it was a curious thing. Perhaps knowing it was temporary helped matters.

The door opened, and for the second time that day, Guy was rendered speechless.

The drab black had been replaced with a gown worthy of a queen. Deep green velvet contoured a pair of ample breasts and tapered to a waist he very much wanted to encircle with his hands. And pull her toward him. Taste the bold woman who was now, if only for a short time, his wife.

"And you were to be a nun." He made a noise in the back of his throat.

"Pardon?"

Was she really so innocent?

Guy spotted her bag next to the bed. Moving past her to take it, his eyes caught the coverlet. Again, he imagined what she'd look like abed. Did she sleep naked or in a shift?

"If God intended for you to be a nun, I am most certainly destined to become the next king of England."

They really should not tarry, but . . .

Guy reached behind his wife and closed the door.

"What are you about?"

He put the bag back down. Took two steps toward her, and stopped.

"It occurs to me Father Wheeland was remiss during the ceremony."

She didn't understand his meaning yet.

"Remiss?"

"In his haste to lead us through the exchange of vows"—he took another step—"he failed to officiate an important part of the ceremony."

"The kiss," she said, biting her succulent bottom lip.

"Aye, my lady."

"We also posted no banns, wear no rings, and do not intend for this arrangement to last."

"We agreed," he argued, taking another step toward her, "this marriage would be consummated."

"You suggested as much. I never agreed to such a thing."

God, his wife was beautiful. That nun's garb did little for her visage, but looking at her now, Guy could almost imagine keeping her.

Almost.

If having a wife, falling in love, were for him. He'd decided long ago that such things were for other people.

But in the meantime . . .

"You will."

He stood as close to her now as he had the eve before, when she'd first blackmailed him. The rose-scented water she must have used to clean drifted between them, a most pleasant scent. Although her expression was quite mutinous, Guy rather liked it. It would make it that much sweeter when she chose to give herself to him. Although he had not lied when he called himself dishonorable, he would never force himself upon a woman. His wife or nay.

Her chest rose and fell in protest. "You would chance a child for a moment of pleasure?"

Guy let his eyes linger on his wife's lips. And then dip lower. When he finally raised his gaze, he answered without pause.

"I would chance much for a moment of pleasure. With you."

Her lips parted.

"You are reckless."

"Aye."

He'd never deny such a claim.

"You should be glad for it," he added, moving back to her bag and lifting it from the ground. "For

certainly no prudent man would allow himself to be blackmailed into marrying a stranger on the same day he proposed treason to one of the most powerful bishops in England."

Striding toward the door, Guy waited for Sabine to join him.

"My lady?"

Instead of walking toward him, she stood, unmoving, in the same spot where he'd nearly kissed her. Dallying for such a purpose had seemed quite reasonable a moment ago. Now, as his mind shifted to the journey ahead, he wondered at his sanity. They needed to leave this place before the pursuit she expected materialized.

"Before we leave . . ."

With his hand on the iron handle of the door, Guy waited for her to finish her sentence.

"Should we not have a plan?"

"For?"

"You make for Noreham Castle to meet with the leader of Bande de Valeur?"

"We," he corrected. "Unless you'd prefer to stay here?"

She shuddered.

"We've not spoken of what happens afterward."

His grip on her bag tightened. "I assumed from the way you so deftly threatened to share my conversation with the bishop that you understood what might happen."

She blinked.

"There may not be an 'afterward,' Sabine. 'Tis as likely Aceline de Chabannes will report me to the king's men as he will turn tail and head back to France. If I leave Noreham Castle with my head intact, then we can indeed discuss the dissolution of this marriage."

"You do not expect to leave Noreham alive."

He shrugged. "If I do, it will be at the expense of alerting the king to our actions. Either way, you will more likely be a widow than find yourself divorced."

"You expect to die?" she repeated.

He opened the door.

"Always. Sooner if you don't come with me," he said, ignoring the fact that it was he who'd first delayed them. Ignoring the fact that, aside from the order and their cause, he almost had something worth living for.

Almost.

For Lady Sabine was not his wife in truth, nor would she ever be.

CHAPTER 9

"They are dead. Both of them."

Sabine didn't believe him. Her father's over-lord was a hard man, but not so callous that he would deliver such news with so little emotion.

"Nay." Her heart began to race, louder and faster until he could likely hear it too. "Nay."

He touched her on the shoulder.

"Sabine?"

"Nay," she repeated, over and over again.

"Sabine?"

Her eyes flew open, the dream lingering with her. Nay, not so much a dream as a memory, one that had haunted her for weeks.

She'd fallen asleep leaning against a tree, an unlikely spot for slumber, although they'd had precious little rest since departing Holybourne Abbey. After leaving the abbey where they'd married, they'd ridden well into the night. When Guy finally signaled it was time to stop, Sabine nearly fell off their mount and embraced the ground. He'd prepared a fire then, and the warmth had lulled her to sleep.

And into a nightmare.

Handing her a piece of meat and a chunk of bread, Guy sat next to her.

Much too close.

That morning, Sabine had thought he intended to make good on his promise to consummate the marriage. Despite having the opportunity, he had not taken advantage of her.

The mercenary was more honorable than she had first imagined, certainly more so than he claimed. Which did not account for her disappointment when he did not so much as claim her lips.

They ate in silence, watching the fire and sitting awkwardly together. Until he handed her a skin of ale. His fingers brushed against her, apurpose.

"What did you dream?"

His tone, devoid of its typical edge, was one of concern. Who *was* this man? The arrogant mercenary she'd met? The brazen traitor she knew him to be? A man who could easily claim her body but instead spoke to her as if he cared for her well-being?

"Why do you ask?"

He took back the skin.

"Are you always so suspicious?"

Her answer to that was immediate. "Aye."

She'd been taught to be so.

She leaned forward, the bark of the tree behind her cutting into the thin linen shift. When Guy had first suggested she remove her travel gown, she'd laughed, thinking him mad. But it had soon become apparent the only possession left to her upon arriving at Holybourne would be quite impractical for this journey, and so Sabine had relented.

Thankfully, it was a sturdy linen, more like a simple gown than a chemise. But it still lacked the layers of material to which she was accustomed in such company.

"If you've little desire to converse, perhaps we should pass the time with other activities?"

Smiling, she took a bite of bread.

"Do you ever relent?" she asked, knowing the answer already.

"If I did"—he placed the skin between them —"you would be dining now with a corpse."

"Has life so mistreated you, then?"

She chanced a glance at him. The wide-open linen shirt gave her pause. Looking away quickly, she stared at the fire instead. He had the body of a mercenary. Not, of course, that she knew any others. But she could imagine it must be a difficult life indeed. And Sabine knew near-constant fighting was the danger to which he referred.

The result: arms nearly as thick as the tree against which she leaned.

"Not at all, my lady. I'm still here, am I not?"

By his standards, Sabine should be thankful she was alive rather than lamenting the life she'd lost the day her parents were both killed.

"I suppose."

"You never answered my question."

An owl's call did so for her. Without realizing it at first, she moved slightly toward her husband. It was the first time Sabine had ever seen such darkness. If not for the fire, she'd not be able to see her own knees tucked up in front of her.

"I dreamt," she said, "of the day I learned my parents were killed."

"A dream you often have?"

How did he know? She finished the food he'd given her, only for it to be immediately replenished.

"Aye," she admitted.

"How were they killed?"

The very idea of telling him would have seemed absurd a few days earlier. None knew of what she was about to share. But Guy was different.

His cause was her own.

Popping the last bit of meat into her mouth, she

reached for the skin. After a long swig of ale, Sabine shifted away from the tree and toward her unwitting husband.

It was time for a bit of truth.

"I suspect they were murdered."

Guy recoiled.

"My father once served as marshal for the king in his youth, at Holgate Castle. When the king was a prince, of course. Even then, my father despised him. Knew the kind of king he would become. The son of a minor baron, he had little land and even less coin. But he had my mother, whom he met at Holgate. And he had me."

Guy listened intently.

"One day, a dear friend of my father's nearly broke down our door with his knocking. I remember it well—the sound awoke me from a deep slumber. He was less than a day's ride ahead of the sheriff's men, coming to arrest him."

"To arrest your father? For what offense?"

"Plotting with Robert Fitzwalter against the king's life."

Guy had obviously not expected that answer.

"He and my mother fled to Lispen Castle in County Durham. I was sent to Lord Burge, my father's overlord, despite begging to go with them. But my father insisted it was too dangerous. There was brief discussion of my mother coming with me, but Burge would never have accepted her. As it was, he resisted taking me as his ward but was shamed into doing so."

"Burge knew why your parents fled?"

She nodded. "Nay. Though he despises John as much as any Northern lord, he would never participate in an open rebellion against the king."

She took a deep breath and forged ahead.

"Less than a fortnight after arriving at Dunham

Castle, I stood in the hall as Burge delivered news of their deaths to me. They were apparently in an accident of some sort. The details have always been murky. I suspect the king's men found them." Sabine tucked her legs up under her. "The dream," she finished weakly.

"I am sorry, Sabine."

Something about the way her name fell from his lips brought forth tears. Sabine had cried for so many days she'd felt hollow by the time she arrived at Holybourne. The emptiness had only retreated due to her desire to escape.

He reached over, wiping away the single tear more tenderly than a mother comforting a newborn babe. Certainly not the reaction she'd expected from the hardened mercenary. Pulling back, Guy sat against the tree.

"You are the daughter of rebels," he said, more to himself than to her.

Sabine smiled for the first time that night.

"Nay, husband." His wide-eyed expression every time she said the word, as if the reminder startled him, made her want to use it more. "Not just the daughter of rebels. You'll not be rid of me until I'm able to do my part in this mission of yours."

His eyes widened.

"John is my king too," she finished, willing him to understand. To accept her support. Not to relegate her, as Lord Burge and the nuns had done, to a role she was not destined to fill.

Guy stood then, pushing away from the tree and extending his hand. And she knew from his slow smile that he actually understood how important it was for her to finish what her parents had started.

Not for the first time, it struck her that she was meant to overhear his conversation with the bishop.

"'Tis well we met," he said, assisting her up. "And I readily accept your offer of assistance."

She took his hand and was almost disappointed he let it go after helping her up. Perhaps she'd misjudged this husband of hers.

"And will gladly accept your other offer as well before we reach Noreham."

"Other offer?"

When he looked back at her, Sabine chastised herself for entertaining such gracious sentiments toward the mercenary. Other offer indeed.

She would see that no such offer was extended. Ever.

The sound of his laughter echoed through the forest around them.

CHAPTER 10

"Married?"

Guy had almost avoided Licheford Castle for this reason. Unfortunately, he needed to speak to Conrad, and his friend's holding was directly in Noreham's path. But Conrad, of course, sought an explanation.

"I will explain later."

He prayed Conrad did not press him. After two days of hard travel, Sabine was in need of a bit of rest. And a bed.

That thought immediately led to another. One that continued to assail him given the close proximity of his wife, the only woman he'd ever met who appeared immune to his charms. Unfortunate, that. Now that Guy knew her story, he no longer begrudged her for the way she'd waylaid him at Holybourne. The opposite, in fact.

He admired the hell out of her.

Conrad, ever the gentleman, had already made his way to Sabine. He saw her glance briefly at the scar that ran from his cheekbone to his jaw. An odd, unidentifiable sensation assaulted him as his friend assisted her in dismounting. The way she looked at him . . .

Of course, she'd admired the castle too, and he could not deny both the holding and the man were grand in every way. Conrad's father had possessed an even more commanding presence. His handshake had been so vigorous, Guy could still feel his grip.

Dismissing the thought, he followed the earl and Sabine into the keep. They climbed a set of stairs, arriving in the great hall moments later. He watched Sabine's face as she stared up at the wall hangings.

Conrad's mother had a passion for embroidery and color. As a result, Licheford Castle had become known for her talent nearly as much as it was for the former earl's temper.

"They are . . . spectacular."

Conrad smiled as he did every time his mother's work was appreciated. They were not all her doing, of course. But her handiwork could be seen throughout the hall. And the hardened knight, now an earl, could not be prouder.

"Thank you. My mother had an affinity for creating them. That one"—he pointed to a bright green banner hanging just behind the dais—"is our family crest. It was her favorite."

It occurred to him then Conrad and Sabine had much in common. Like Sabine, Conrad had also lost both parents, in their case within a sennight of each other. Although the culprit had been more apparent in his case—his parents had succumbed to a mysterious illness that had nearly claimed him as well. A dark time in Saint-Clair history.

"'Tis lovely. You must have been very proud."

Conrad studied Sabine just a bit too intently for Guy's taste. "Indeed," he said, pointing to her waist. "Your own creation?"

What the hell was Conrad pointing at?

"Indeed."

Sabine's hands moved to the embroidered belt

around her waist. Leather with bits of ribbon hanging from the ends. He had noticed the unusual piece but had not remarked on it.

"My mother taught me, as her mother did before her. Though she is no longer with me"—she let go of the belt—"I very much hope to carry on the tradition."

"A girdler, then?"

Sabine nodded. "I hope to find a guild that will take me."

Conrad looked at him then. Guy did not know what to say. He hadn't even known Sabine was in possession of such a skill, let alone that she'd made the belt herself. Somehow, however, Conrad had known.

He must have learned to decipher such things in his training as an earl. Whatever the case, it gave him an unfair advantage. Sabine was practically beaming at him.

Pretending not to care, he shrugged and walked away. Let Conrad take care of his wife, then. The earl was clearly better equipped to do so. Mumbling about leaving them to their conversation, he accepted a mug of ale from one of the serving girls preparing the midday meal.

A castle of this size never saw less than fifty men in the hall during meals, sometimes more. And when Conrad was not in attendance, it ran seamlessly without him, courtesy of the steward who had been at Licheford for as many years as Conrad was alive.

Guy looked over his shoulder just in time to see that very steward, Ansel, escort Sabine from the hall. He was a good man who would treat her well.

"Start talking."

Conrad's deep voice did not terrify him as it did most men. But neither did it make him feel at ease. As Guy followed his friend into a corridor that led to the solar, he drank deeply, nearly finishing his ale.

Once inside the chamber, a smaller replica of the great hall but larger than most solars, Guy sank into the seat across from Conrad's desk. The leather seat accommodated him nicely.

"I thought I might miss you," Guy said conversationally. "How was your journey to Wayfair?"

Judging from the set of Conrad's jaw, he was not inclined to answer.

"Very well. She overheard my conversation with the bishop at Holybourne. Threatened to divulge the details unless I helped her escape." He was actually looking forward to sharing this next bit of information. "She didn't wish to become a nun, you see."

"A nun? You married a nun?"

Guy didn't even attempt to hold back a smile.

"Not quite."

"Not . . ." Conrad took a deep breath, something he often did to calm his otherwise volatile temper. "Not quite?"

"An oblate," he admitted. "And against her will."

Conrad leaned forward. "So you truly married her?"

Guy still had difficulty reconciling that particular fact, but there was no denying it, and so he nodded.

"Her father was Robert de Stuteville, lord of Cottingham. Do you know of him?"

Conrad's posture changed immediately. "Aye. Some said he colluded with Fitzwalter."

"They would be correct. He did. Was hunted down and killed by John's men. And his wife too. Sabine was sent to Lord Burge, Cottingham's overlord, who promptly sold her off to Holybourne."

He could see Conrad working out the rest of it in his head.

"She worried he might come for her."

"Aye."

"Were you followed?"

"Nay."

"Shite." He paused, then added, "You were careless to allow for such a conversation to be overheard."

Thinking back, as he'd done many times over the past few days, Guy very much agreed. He had relied on the Reverend Mother to secure their meeting place, a rather foolish mistake. "Perhaps. But it doesn't change the circumstances. Besides, her father may have attempted to do away with the king, which makes Sabine an ally in this endeavor."

Guy didn't like the look Conrad gave him.

"That's the second time since you arrived you've shown affection toward the woman. But this marriage is not a true one?"

"Nay, it is not," he replied, too quickly. "Not at all. I will ensure Burge understands her new position. Actually, you will help with that part of my plan. And once I finish my business with Bande de Valeur, she and I will part ways."

Conrad crossed his arms and grunted but gave no other response.

"She is a smart woman. No doubt she has a plan. Relatives, perhaps, who will keep her safe."

Conrad laughed then, and the sound grated. "You haven't spoken with her yet about her future plans?"

"I don't suppose the bishop's support of our cause, and the funds he's offered to send de Chabannes and his company back to France, warrant any attention?"

Conrad didn't answer. Finally, after an uncomfortably long silence, he sat back, the wooden seat creaking beneath his weight. He understood Guy's meaning and, thankfully, did not seem inclined to harass him further on the subject of his wife.

"I'm glad to hear it," Conrad said. "And we've Lord Wayfair's support as well. Although he worries

John's rumored promise of another battle will rouse support for him from some of the southern barons."

It was always as such. Those closest to the king in proximity were more inclined to accept his wayward tactics. They'd hoped the last wave of tax increases, along with the loss at Bouvines, for which the money had been raised, would sway opinion, even in the south. And yet, the barons to the south seemed inclined to see another battle.

"If they continue to support John after Bouvines, they are as foolish as the king."

"You might keep that opinion contained to this chamber."

"I'm not the one who cares what others think of me."

Conrad snorted. "You'd make a fine earl indeed."

It was a jest between them, and the other members of their order, that Guy had been born into the exact perfect position for him. He craved adventure, was touted as one of the greatest swordsmen in England, and would have difficulty bowing down to any overlord.

Even the king.

"Enough talk and more drink."

He stood, Conrad following suit.

"Very well. But I have just one more question about"—Conrad cleared his throat—"your wife."

CHAPTER 11

Sabine pretended to be asleep. It seemed the most prudent thing to do as she waited for Guy to arrive. Conrad—the earl had insisted she use his given name—assumed she and Guy would share a chamber, a reasonable assumption for a man and wife.

Although certainly he must understand their circumstances? He had named the earl as a co-conspirator, as "more than a friend." Wouldn't he confide in such a man? But Guy hadn't objected to the sleeping arrangements.

On the road, he had insisted on giving her his bedroll—the only one they had. He was a mystery, this temporary husband of hers. Crude one moment, noble the next.

I will gladly accept your other offer as well before we reach Noreham.

She said she'd not offer herself to him, and she'd meant it. But the way he looked at her . . . Sabine couldn't help but wonder what it would feel like to relent to desire.

A reckless thought.

The door opened.

Although her back was to the door, she listened as

he removed his boots, but she could not discern what else he may have removed. A splash of water and then silence. Had he used the sage and salt mixture that had been provided? And the linen strip of cloth for his teeth? Had he taken off his hose or tunic? Surely he would not sleep in the nude, as many were wont to do, with her in the same bed.

Finally, when she could no longer take the suspense, the feather bed sagged with his weight.

"You are awake, my lady?"

How had he surmised as much?

"If you'd like to discuss your offer now . . ."

"I made no offer," she said, turning.

Although the room was lit only by candlelight, she could see his face clearly.

"How did you know?" she asked, stumbling over the last word. Though he was covered, Guy's shoulders and arms were bare. Thick but well-defined muscles moved in tandem as he turned on his side toward her.

"That you were awake or that you were considering making an offer?"

His ever-present grin was nearly impossible to resist. Despite herself, Sabine felt the corners of her mouth tugging upward.

"That I was awake. I am most certainly not considering any offer."

"Your breathing," he said, staring straight at her lips. "It was much too fast, though not nearly as fast as it will be if you decide to engage in our marital responsibilities."

What would it be like to kiss such a man?

"As we do not plan to stay married, it seems a risky proposal," she countered. "At least for one whose belly could easily swell with a babe."

Even though she was completely covered by her

nondescript shift, as well as a soft linen coverlet, Sabine felt naked beneath his gaze.

"That is your only concern?"

His eyes locked on hers.

"One of many."

She didn't move as Guy reached over, his fingers brushing her shoulder as he lifted a few errant strands of her hair.

Sabine's chest rose and fell as she waited for him to move his hand away. Instead, he began to twirl the hair about his fingers, never taking his eyes from hers.

"There are ways to ensure that does not happen."

Sabine knew as much from her mother, who had been unusually free with her knowledge.

"There are other concerns as well."

He continued to wrap her hair around his fingers.

"Such as?"

"It would not do well for us to form an attachment."

His abrupt laughter pained her more than it should.

"I am sorry." He stopped, but not before the sound was ingrained in her ears. "I forget you hardly know me at all."

"And if I did?" she bit back, annoyed.

"You would know I do not form attachments. To anyone."

He lied. "Not even to your order?"

His hand froze.

"Do you forget I heard . . . everything?" Perhaps she had pushed too hard. Or perhaps not hard enough.

"They do not hold me back."

"As a wife would?"

"Aye."

Certainly to hear him say so aloud was a relief.

The last thing she'd set out to find was a husband in truth—a man to contain her. And yet . . .

His fingers continued their ministrations, the gentle tug somehow soothing.

"From fighting for coin?"

His eyes narrowed. "'Tis what I do. Who I am."

She hadn't meant for it to sound like a judgement, but he'd obviously taken it as such.

"I have . . . plans."

The words seemed forced, as if he were sharing a difficult admission. But he'd told her nothing of his plans.

"As do I," she admitted.

His eyes dropped down, and once again, she felt exposed. She'd never lain like this with a man, side by side in a bed.

"A girdler?"

She raised her chin, unapologetic.

"Aye. 'Tis not unheard of for a woman. My mother and her mother before her made belts, and I've always imagined doing so for coin. If I can find a guild . . ."

She stopped, feeling foolish.

Letting her hair drop, Guy moved his hand away, adjusting the pillow beneath him. He seemed more inclined to speak with her than to sleep, and she had to admit she was rather enjoying this time together. But his easy manner and good looks distracted her, and Sabine could not afford to become distracted. She had a suspicion that, if she were not vigilant, this man would remove the barriers she'd put between them before she even realized he'd done so.

"If you find a guild, they will no doubt be impressed with your craft. And 'tis a fine occupation for a lady such as yourself."

No words could have surprised her more.

"You truly believe so?"

He did not hesitate.

"I do."

She wasn't sure what to say.

"After we convince Bande de Valeur to return to France, you will help me find one, a guild, before we part ways?"

"We?"

Sabine feigned innocence. "I thought you understood. I would do my part in this rebellion of yours. In my father's good name."

"Do you have no other family to go to?"

Sabine sighed. "I'd have appealed to them if I did. Neither of my parents had siblings, and neither of their parents live. When Burge received my wardship, my father's lands naturally reverted back to the crown."

"Naturally."

"My own title is a courtesy one only, given the circumstances."

He seemed oddly happy at that news. Turning onto his back, Guy sighed and closed his eyes. Although she was tired too, she could not resist asking, "That pleases you?"

He did not stir.

"Aye."

"Why?"

His lips turned up ever so slowly, though he did not open his eyes.

"The things I plan to do with you are hardly appropriate for a lady."

His eyes finally opened and sought hers.

"Sabine."

Heart hammering in her chest, Sabine knew she should respond, but no words formed on her lips.

"You've simply to make an offer, and I promise"— he winked—"not to refuse."

She couldn't find the words to respond, but

Sabine did have a pillow. She smacked him in the middle of the chest with it, ignoring his laughter and renewing the vow she'd made to herself. If for no other reason than that offering anything to this man would be the epitome of foolishness.

CHAPTER 12

"A word, my lady?" the Earl of Licheford called to her.

They stood just outside the keep. Guy had left to retrieve their horses for their journey to Noreham. He'd warned her they would be on the road for several nights. There was an inn along the way, he explained, but it catered more to mercenaries than lords and ladies. She supposed he was trying to protect her, but if she would risk her life at Noreham, she could certainly brave a simple inn.

"Of course," she told Conrad, for she surely couldn't deny him.

"Thank you for your hospitality," she said, watching as Guy emerged from the stables. "And for the fine riding gown. The maid would not let me refuse—"

"As I instructed her to do. You look lovely in it. My mother's tailor made her so many gowns there are several she never had occasion to wear."

The maid had arrived at her door with it that morning, telling her much the same story. Sabine had tried to send her away, but the woman had been quite insistent on helping her into it.

"I thank you again, my lord."

Conrad angled toward her, his expression turning serious.

"Be patient with him."

She did not have to ask for clarification.

"He would have you believe he cares for little, including you."

Sabine must have appeared startled, for Conrad immediately apologized.

"I do not mean to be so crude, but there is little time for courtesy. I've known him for many years. Being a friend to Guy Lavallis takes some measure of patience. I can only imagine being his wife will take more so."

"He did not explain the circumstances of our marriage?"

Conrad chuckled. "He did. And I dare say he is impressed with your craftiness. As am I."

Sabine didn't know what to say.

"He was raised by a man even harder than the one who strides toward us. His mother, a Frenchwoman, left them both at an early age, and I do not believe Guy ever really recovered."

Sabine looked from Conrad to her husband, who spoke to a stablehand as they led the horses forward.

"How awful." He had mentioned his mother was French, but now that she thought on it, it was the only thing he'd said about her. To abandon your only child . . .

"He was raised by mercenaries, never in one place for long."

"His father, he is dead as well?"

To her surprise, Conrad shook his head. "Nay. Though where he is, none, including Guy, know."

How . . . odd.

"I tell you this for a reason."

She suspected the reason but said nothing, waiting patiently for him to continue.

"Guy says he craves adventure. Indeed, he doesn't quail from danger. But he is a good man. I'd not align myself with him otherwise."

Sabine was honored he'd trusted her enough to say so.

"I will try to remember that, my lord."

"Conrad. And please do. I hope the knowledge brings you comfort in the trying times ahead."

Trying times indeed. But after the loss of her parents, Sabine felt prepared for anything.

Conrad extended his hand, fist clenched. Sabine looked down at it in confusion.

"My wrist," he said. And so she gently clasped her hand around his wrist. "Your father gave his life for a cause we continue to fight. You pledged yourself to that same cause. As such, you are a member of the Order of the Broken Blade. Be safe on your travels."

Sabine did not understand the words, exactly, but she knew from his expression something important had just happened. Guy's order. Had Conrad really just made her a member?

"I am not a knight," she said, knowing a bit about such orders.

"Then an honorary member, if it pleases you."

She tightened her grip as much as was possible around his thick wrist.

"It pleases me very much."

Conrad nodded.

Sabine dropped her hand.

So intent was she on Conrad's gesture that she hadn't realized Guy had joined them. He stood to the side, looking at them with wide, approving eyes.

"Take care," Conrad said. "She is one of us now."

For the second time in as many days, Sabine could not think of an adequate response. It had been so very long since she'd felt a part of anything. Reaching for the reins of the horse Conrad had pledged to her, she smiled to the earl.

"I will do my best," she said, deliberately misunderstanding. "But he promises to be a stubborn one."

Without waiting for assistance, Sabine mounted easily, enjoying Conrad's laughter at her insinuation she would take care of Guy.

A ridiculous notion, to be sure. If there ever lived a man who could care for himself, it was her husband, Guy Lavallis of Cradney Wrens.

❧

"DON'T MOVE."

Guy knew the bastards riding toward them. He was surprised they hadn't encountered more of the sort before now. It would take them at least a fortnight to reach Noreham Castle along the eastern coast. In that time, he expected to meet more than one party that would attempt to rob them. Such was the way of travel on these roads. As usual, he'd avoided the most well-used routes, knowing such pathways were favored by the king's men—and also Lord Burge —but these remote roads carried other dangers.

"Hold," the sellsword called out, obviously not recognizing him. "I said hold."

Before he could shout again, Guy had sped up enough to grab the man's reins. Not two years earlier, this very same man, Dimmock St. James, had lost a match to Terric at the Tournament of the North. The dullard had failed to deliver the spoils. Terric would have refused to take the man's horse—he had no need of it—but he never had the chance.

"Or better yet, dismount and put up your sword," he called, seeing the exact moment the other man recognized him.

St. James, a heavily bearded man, laughed as if Guy jested with him.

"What say you?" St. James said to his two companions. "Shall I engage in swordplay with Guy Lavallis?" He didn't wait for an answer. "Nay. I think I'll allow you to pass instead."

"Dismount," he growled. "And put up your sword. Or they"—he gestured to the men—"will be without a leader by the time we leave this clearing."

It was near dark, but Guy could easily see the other men's faces. They, at least, would not interfere. Smart men. He glanced toward Sabine, who thankfully did not appear scared. Merely curious.

St. James hesitated but finally dismounted.

Hand on his hilt, Guy stepped forward.

"I will be taking what you owe Terric Kennaugh from when you last met."

St. James drew his sword, so Guy did the same.

"I owe the bastard Scot nothing."

Guy yelled back to Sabine, "Turn away," and took another step forward.

"A Scot, aye," he continued to taunt St. James, "but one with more honor than a thousand of your kind."

The insult hit its mark. Though his eyes were on St. James, Guy watched the man's two companions in his periphery. He fully expected to fight all three before the day was done. A shame his wife would have to witness such a spectacle, but it could not be helped. St. James had cheated his friend and would answer for it.

"My kind? It seems we are in good company, *routier*."

"If you intended to insult me, you missed your mark, St. James."

It was true, he had run with the famed band of

specialized mercenaries for a time in France. He was anything but ashamed by the association.

"I wonder, Lavallis," St. James smirked. "Will your lady be glad to be rid of you?"

He did not let the taunt goad him. Guy would prefer not to fight in front of Sabine, but he could not let the slight against Terric pass.

"Put your sword down, pay the debt, and you may ride away with your companions."

"I owe no debt to a Scotsman," St. James sneered.

Guy was finished negotiating. He lunged at his opponent, and St. James deflected the blow at the last moment. They began to circle each other in the clearing, parrying their swords.

There was a reason St. James had been paired with Terric in a final match at the tourney. The man was skilled, and he matched Guy's every swing and thrust as his companions dismounted. They likely did not think he saw them approaching, so when one slowly sauntered around Guy's back, he assumed the worst of the man's intentions.

Still engaging St. James, he waited to be sure the man truly intended to come at him from the rear. He wore only a padded gambeson, and though it may deflect a blow to the back, it would not save him if the man went for his neck.

By God's own nails, the bastard truly did intend to stab him in the back . . .

He quickly adjusted his grip on the sword, bringing it under his arm, and thrust it into his adversary. Removing the sword just as quickly, he lifted it in front of him just in time to block a blow that would have beheaded him.

Turning to bring both men into view, Guy took advantage of St. James's momentary confusion as he watched his man fall to the ground. Lifting his sword for a death blow, he stopped at the last moment. St.

James had thrown his hands into the air, and his sword landed on the ground with a thud.

Both St. James and his surviving companion bent over the dead man. Guy had killed many men in his lifetime and could have told them he was, in fact, no longer for this world. If the man had not attempted to stab him in the back . . . if he'd worn proper armor . . . or if St. James had not refused to pay his debt . . . it mattered not.

The man was dead.

Standing, St. James bent down to pick up his sword.

"Leave the sword and the man's mount. And I shall call the chief of Clan Kennaugh's debt fulfilled."

His voice was hard, his gaze even more so. Guy waited to see if St. James would sacrifice two more lives for his stubbornness.

Thankfully, he did not.

For the first time since the fight had erupted, Guy chanced a look back at Sabine. He could not discern her expression, but she was safe. Nothing else mattered.

When St. James moved to leave, Guy nodded to his fallen companion in disgust.

"You would leave him there, on the road?"

Exchanging a glance and a near-identical grunt of displeasure, St. James and his man reluctantly lifted the fallen sellsword from the ground. Guy picked up St. James's sword and hastened to Sabine and his abandoned horse. He mounted and guided Sabine past the men.

St. James's question floated up to him.

"The horse?"

"I've changed my mind. Keep it. I've no use for him where I am headed."

With that, they rode away from the ill-fated clearing, regret for the loss of life bubbling inside him. He would have much preferred to kill the man responsible for that day's events. Guy looked at Sabine then, listening for any sounds to indicate they were being followed.

"Are you well?"

She did not seem so. His wife's face was devoid of color.

Sabine shook her head. "You . . . you were nearly killed."

Guy laughed, not meaning to sound callous but unable to hold back his reaction.

"Nay, wife. Not nearly so. If I had thought for a moment my life was at risk, I would not have engaged the man. I'd not leave you unprotected on the road."

She blinked. "But . . . there were three of them. And . . ."

He waited, but she never finished the thought.

"I was never in danger," he assured her. "I'm sorry you had to witness such a thing. But there was no help for it. That bastard St. James lost a match to Terric but failed to forfeit his prize. 'Twas too dishonorable an act to be overlooked."

"Honor," she murmured. "A quality you yourself claim not to possess."

He could not deny it.

"I believe, husband, you are not quite who you claim to be."

Another statement he could not deny.

"But I aim to learn who you are before this journey has ended."

CHAPTER 13

To Sabine's surprise, Guy stopped at the inn after all. Although small villages usually grew around castles or chapels, like mushrooms on a log, there were none nearby. This village consisted of only ten or so structures, a waterwheel, and the stone building where Guy had stopped.

The Fiddler's Inn.

A wooden sign hung from its roof, creaking as it swayed back and forth in the wind. As they moved closer, Sabine realized a wooden bridge connected the inn to another building similarly appointed. Stone-bottomed with a second floor made of wood and thatched roofs, it looked slightly odd and disproportional, but as the September sun began to set, the light emanating from within made it quite appealing.

"I thought we were not stopping here?" she asked, allowing Guy to assist her down.

They'd not spoken much since the incident, the ride uneventful for the remainder of the afternoon.

Guy continued to hold her hand once she was on the ground, much to her relief, and she allowed herself to grip his fingers.

"Any woman who witnessed what you did earlier

63

today and kept such calm . . . Fiddler's will be as tame as an abbey."

He did let go then, and Sabine immediately felt the loss of his touch.

"I am not so unaffected as it would seem," she admitted. Earlier in the day, Sabine had started shaking at the thought of that man lying on the ground, unmoving. The unsteady feeling had eventually subsided, but the swiftness with which he'd died . . .

She hadn't even had time to warn Guy. The scream had stuck in her throat even as she watched the man stalk behind him.

"Many thanks," Guy said to a stablehand who took their mounts. He slipped the man a coin and then reclaimed her hand, threading their fingers together.

"Here, we are man and wife in truth."

For a moment she misunderstood his meaning. He seemed to realize it, for he leaned toward her and whispered, "Anytime, my lady. I await your pleasure."

Her breath caught at his words. Until a waft of stale ale assaulted her as Guy opened the front door. For a village so small, the hall of the inn was certainly bustling. Nearly every table was occupied. To her eyes, the place resembled a tavern more than an inn. Of course, she'd only stayed at one other inn, many years ago, so she did not have much basis for comparison.

When everyone in the room turned to look at them, Sabine had the momentary urge to hide behind Guy. But she'd promised herself she would not besmirch her parent's memory by being any less fearless, strong, and loyal than they had been.

While it appeared she was the only woman in the room, she would not be ashamed of it. Nor would she let anyone frighten her because of it.

They would have you believe they have something you

do not possess. But 'tis not the truth, Sabine. A woman brings life into the world. Remember that.

Reminding herself of her mother's words, her mother's strength, Sabine tried not to grip Guy's arm too tightly. Besides, she would be alone someday, navigating situations like this one. She could not allow herself to rely on Guy.

"If anyone yells at you, ignore them. If they touch you, tell me."

Sabine hated that his words brought her such comfort. She didn't want to need him.

An especially burly man, a knight by the look of him, gave her the exact kind of glance Guy knew she'd receive. An appreciative one, tinged with a slight sneer.

At that exact moment, her husband stepped between them, Guy towering above the other man, who was seated at a table with several others. She couldn't see either of their faces now, but the knight's companions were well within her view. There were four of them, making her wonder if Guy valued his life at all. He really did seem inclined to seek out quarrelsome situations.

"You'll be wanting to give your ale more attention than my wife."

Guy rested his hand on his sheathed sword.Others around them stopped talking and looked their way.

"You'll be wanting to move along," the man mocked. He and all of his companions stood, but Guy did not move. Sabine, on the other hand, backed away enough to see her husband's face. She shivered, unaccustomed to seeing him so serious. Nay, not just serious.

Deadly.

"You'll all be wanting to sit down," another voice

yelled from the other side of the table. "'Tis Guy Lavallis, you fools."

Sabine had thought for sure she was about to watch yet another fight, but at those words, the men who'd threatened them, including the one who had looked at her, sat like obedient schoolboys.

Still Guy did not move away.

When the men returned to their ales, he lingered a moment longer before taking her hand and leading her to the far side of the hall.

A small empty table beckoned. When they sat, a woman immediately appeared with a pitcher and two mugs. Where had she come from? Sabine had not seen a serving girl, or any other women, earlier.

Guy poured both of them an ale and drank deeply from his mug.

She simply stared.

"What happened back there?"

His smile had returned, as if he'd not just almost gotten killed.

"I ensured your safety this night, lady wife."

Her brows raised. "Safety? Would it not have been better to seat ourselves unnoticed? You are, after all, alone. That man was a knight and had at least four companions with him."

Guy leaned forward, the hints of green in his brown eyes twinkling. A lone candle, paired with the moonlight streaming inside from the window next to them, cast an almost ethereal glow on an otherwise hardened man.

Until he smiled.

Now he looked like any other. Nay, most men didn't look like Guy Lavallis, more was the pity, but the cold glint in his eyes was gone and he no longer looked like a killer.

"I am also a knight. Sir Guy, at your service, my lady."

"I suppose I've not thought of you in this light, as a knight, despite knowing otherwise. This is the first you've used your title."

"The title is meaningless. It is a man's training that defines him."

"How does someone like . . . how does a mercenary become a knight?"

"A story for another day. As to your second question? Nay. 'Twould not have been better for us to avoid a confrontation. You're still attracting attention. It was inevitable someone would attempt to dishonor you. Now, at least, we will not be bothered."

"Not be . . ." She stared, incredulous. "You are but one man."

"Thankfully, one man who has been in the employ of at least two lords who grace this hall. One who has participated in enough tournaments to be known by reputation. One man, aye. But if they're willing to forget I'm just a man, I'm happy to let them. Their stories shall keep us safe."

"Stories about your exploits?"

Guy pushed the other mug toward her. "Aye."

"What have you done in these tourneys, or as a mercenary, that would seat an entire retinue of knights? Surely together they could have overcome you?"

"Surely not." He winked. "Drink."

So she did. Sabine tried to imagine what they knew of Guy that she did not. She thought back to earlier in the day, to the moment she'd thought she was about to become a widow. Even now, she struggled to understand the sheer speed with which he'd swung his sword under his arm to slay his opponent. Sabine had attempted to lift her father's broadsword before and knew the strength it took to do so. How strong was he, then, to enact such a feat?

Her eyes fell on his arm, now lifted for another

drink. She'd seen those arms bare and could imagine the strength they possessed.

Guy caught her looking.

"Are you always so well-pleased with yourself?"

"Aye."

He answered so quickly, Sabine knew the opposite to be true. But she remained silent.

The serving girl plopped two meat pies in front of them.

"The only fare left this eve."

The girl's gaze lingered on Guy. She did not even attempt to hide her appreciation for what she saw.

If Guy could dissuade roaming eyes, then Sabine could do the same.

"My *husband* and I thank you for the meal, and for our privacy."

The girl stood up straight, frowning, and walked away.

Guy's laugh prompted her to cross her arms in front of her.

"Your tongue is as sharp as my sword."

"I will thank you not to laugh at your wife, *Sir Guy*."

He cleared his throat, still smiling.

Uncrossing her arms, Sabine took a bite of the pie. After a day of riding, she was so very hungry.

"My tongue," she said between bites, "is none of your concern."

Leaning forward, Guy opened his mouth and touched his own tongue to his top lip. Slowly. Deliberately.

Sabine forgot to breathe.

"Alas, your tongue is very much my concern."

Elbows on the table, he leaned even closer. "If you would but make your offer, I could show you exactly how it is so, my lady wife."

Lord help her, Sabine very much wanted to learn of what he spoke.

"I told you," she ground out, "no such offer will be forthcoming."

Guy sat back, lifted his fork, and began to eat. But this wasn't just about sating his appetite. Nay, he lingered over every bite. Once he licked his lips, allowing Sabine to see the pink tip of his tongue.

Her core clenched as it had never done before. She wondered at her stubborn refusal to indulge herself. This man was her husband, was he not? Would it not be permissible to give in to this small temptation?

Nay!

Intimacy between them would not end well.

Instead of answering, she continued to eat. It struck her that Guy had been quite correct in his assessment of the situation. Although a few people glanced their way, they garnered far less attention than when they'd first entered.

"Who are you?" she blurted.

"I have many monikers, my lady. But that of your husband is my current favorite."

Sabine rolled her eyes.

"When we met, I thought you an arrogant bastard," Sabine admitted.

"When we met . . ." He took a swig of ale and clanked the mug back onto the table. "I thought you a nun."

"An easy enough assumption, given the circumstances."

Sabine finished the meat pie, peering up at Guy occasionally.

"What do you want to know?" he answered finally.

She had so many questions, but she kept coming back to the question of his knighthood.

"All right. How does a mercenary come to be knighted?" she tried asking again.

"It was the year of our Lord twelve hundred and six," he said with a flourish. Sabine shook her head gently at his antics. "An invasion by your king saw me fighting for Philip at La Rochelle. The very same man knighted me on the battlefield after a hard-fought victory."

She could not have been more surprised. "You fought for France?"

"Aye."

"Against England?"

"'Tis what I said."

"But . . . now you risk your life to protect the very country you fought against. I don't understand."

"'Tis the life of a mercenary." He shrugged. "Philip pays well. As does John, which is why my . . ." She shot him a look. ". . . Our mission will not be an easy one."

"But you are not getting paid for this."

"I am not. This particular mission is for the order."

"But why? Why would a man loyal to no one risk everything for three Englishmen—"

"Two Englishmen. And a Scotsman."

"If you care not about the outcome?"

Guy turned serious. She'd hit upon something he did not want to discuss. Interesting.

"A story for another day."

Sabine looked around the inn's hall. "We've time for it now."

But she could tell Guy was finished talking.

"Nay, we do not." He stood, outstretching his hand. "'Tis time to secure lodgings and"—he smiled—"for us to become husband and wife in truth."

Her heart skipped a beat. "But you said . . ."

She stopped, taking his hand, belatedly realizing

he was teasing her. Sabine tried to summon relief but instead there was only disappointment. Silly, as it was she who had determined their course. The look he was giving her at that very moment served as the only reminder she needed that, given her acquiescence, their marriage would be immediately consummated.

CHAPTER 14

Guy opened the door to their room for the second time that evening. After securing it earlier, he'd left to check on the horses. And to ensure the men whom he'd tangled with earlier had moved on. He'd begun to return, changed his mind, and went to the hall instead.

He'd do better to wait for Sabine to fall asleep.

He found himself distracted by her lips. By the way she breathed in so deeply whenever she was worried. That was how he'd known she was uncomfortable as they entered the inn's hall earlier. Hell, he'd felt much the same way. The Fiddler's Inn was not intended for noblewomen.

But it could be for a girdler. The very idea of it . . .

Guy shook his head. She would be good at the trade, of that he had no doubt. Her work spoke for itself. But would such a life suit Sabine? Although she was certainly resourceful—the manner of their meeting had taught him that—she was also very much a lady. Refined and well-spoken. Heart-wrenchingly beautiful. Nay, he could not imagine her living in a town alone, selling her wares alongside the type of men who would sooner steal from her than they would help her succeed.

That kind of thinking was the exact reason Guy stayed belowstairs for longer than necessary. He was becoming much too entangled with his wife. She was more thoughtful than he, as Guy knew the reason she did not give in to the temptation they both felt. He would do well to follow her lead.

And concentrate on the mission ahead.

The door creaked much too loudly as it opened. The room he'd secured was small but well-appointed. Or tidy, at least. The bed was too small for them both unless he wanted to sleep nearly on top of her.

His cock answered the call. Because aye, he did want that. Very much.

"Guy?"

She sat up. Her voice was not that of a woman who had been sleeping.

"You're awake," he said without looking toward the bed. Best not to tempt himself.

Sabine didn't answer, but he could feel her watching him. Removing his boots, then his tunic and hose, Guy moved to the wooden washstand. Grateful for the bowl of water, more so than he'd expected, he washed himself, remembering only belatedly the drying cloth was in his saddlebag.

"Here."

He turned to Sabine's outstretched hand. She was sitting up in the bed in the same shift she'd worn the night before. He moved toward her, not daring to think of her parted lips as a sign. But when she lifted her neck, he was powerless to prevent his eyes from lingering on the creamy skin there.

Guy deliberately allowed his fingers to linger as they brushed hers. Grasping the cloth, he turned away, but not before he gave his wife a knowing look. One that told her what he wanted. Despite everything that had happened that day, or maybe because of it, he wanted *her*.

So much death, always.

As he dried himself off, Guy thought of the man he'd slain that day. It was little consolation his own life would have been forfeit had he not reacted so quickly. Death was death. And it mattered little that he had seen it often. Each and every one haunted him, even the nameless faces of men on the battlefield.

Such was the life of a mercenary. At least the order's cause was just. He would gladly fight for it, die for it.

Finished, Guy took out his bedroll and placed it on the floor, avoiding Sabine's gaze. The more he looked at her, the less he would be able to resist her.

"You'd sleep on the floor?"

Cursing under his breath, he muttered an affirmation.

"'Tis unnecessary. There is space here, beside me."

Guy looked up then, and even in the dim moonlight streaming into the room through the sole window, he knew that look.

Sabine's eyes fluttered upward, but it was too late.

"What exactly are you offering, Sabine?"

He deliberately drew out her name, his meaning clear.

"A bed to sleep in."

"Nothing more? 'Tis a small bed."

"Nay. Nothing more."

Though he admired her bravado, Guy nearly laughed at her expression as he moved toward her. Did she think he would decline the offer? Had she made it expecting him to do so?

"Many thanks," he said, as formally as he could.

Lying next to her, as he expected, their bodies kissed in a way they had not. Her legs, her hips . . . but still he would not relent until she did so first.

"Good night, Sabine."

Though he closed his eyes, Guy knew sleep would not come. If he had not slept the previous night, knowing she lay beside him in the large bed, or the night before that, lying beneath the stars with her, he certainly could not manage it now. He had a feeling he'd not sleep until they parted.

A thought he wished to avoid.

"Guy?"

He smiled, eyes still closed.

"Aye, my lady wife?"

"You are . . . quite large."

He knew she referred to their close proximity but could not let the comment pass.

"So you did stare overly long at my braies? I thought as much. Thank you for saying so."

He waited. It didn't take long.

"I did not mean—"

Opening his eyes and spinning toward her, Guy propped himself up on his elbow. The sight of her auburn tresses, tumbling down around her breasts, was too great a temptation, and he took hold of a lock, twirling it gently around his fingers. His hand brushed against a very full breast with each twirl.

"I knew to what you referred," he admitted.

"Why do you do that?"

He allowed his hand to linger on her covered breast a bit longer each time he wrapped her hair around his fingers. Inching closer and closer to the center of the mound, he finally found his mark. As he'd expected, her nipple hardened beneath his hand.

"I love the color of your hair, the feel of it beneath my fingers. When it was covered, I imagined it would be a soft brown. But nay, this suits you more. Bold, like my lady wife."

She swallowed.

"Not that." Her eyes begged him not to make her say the words, so he relented and did it for her.

"Ahh, you mean, why do I allow my finger to caress your hardened nipple with each pass?"

Pink stained both of her fair cheeks. "Aye."

Dropping the pretense of toying with her hair, though he did enjoy doing so, Guy tossed the tresses aside so he might lavish his attention on Sabine's breasts. He rubbed his thumb back and forth, easily feeling her arousal even through the linen shift, then took her nipple between his fingers and pinched, ever so slightly.

"You said you would wait until I offered myself to you," she said.

"Mmmm . . ." He cupped her then, nearly overwhelmed by the need to do so without any offending material between them. "I do believe you already did?"

Her eyes widened.

"The very night you asked for me to take you." He clarified, "The night you blackmailed me."

Leaning toward her, so close he could smell the mint on her breath, Guy removed his hand from her chest.

"Does that mean . . ."

Again, she did not put what she wanted into words. No matter, he had plenty of words for what he would like them to do together.

"Does that mean I will finally taste the sweetness of your lips? Continue my exploration of your body, your breasts? Or that I will slide into you and then spend this night making love to the woman who is already mine, in the eyes of both God and man?"

He almost felt sorry for her.

Guy should not do this. His words tortured both of them. By God's own nails, he had never wanted anything more than to do every last thing he'd just described.

But she would ask for it.

Sabine nodded.

And because he was a bastard, Guy opened his mouth and very deliberately licked his lips, wetting them. "Nay," he said, waiting for her reaction. "I'd not hold you to that early offer. 'Twas made out of desperation."

Lying back down, he forced his eyes to close once more.

"Next time, I'd have the offer be made out of desire instead."

He smiled at the strangled sound his dear wife made.

CHAPTER 15

Sabine had never felt less refreshed. Sitting up, she groaned. Guy was gone.

The light streaming in through the window alerted her to the hour, but although she'd slept later than usual, she hadn't slept much. It had taken her most of the night to drift off to sleep. Even after Guy's breathing had turned slow and steady with sleep, she'd lain awake, shocked that he'd found rest when she could not.

At one point, he'd shifted toward her in his sleep, and Sabine could not resist staring at him. His features looked so much softer in sleep. Lips that he'd wet, no doubt intentionally, luring her in as she watched. Her eyes had wandered lower, to the marking on his arm she'd always wondered about, a fleur-de-lis etched in black. Sabine watched as his muscles shifted beneath his flesh every time he moved.

And then something unexpected happened—he pulled her toward him in his sleep, bringing her close until her head was cradled on his shoulder. She allowed it because it felt so very natural, and because he didn't seem to know he'd done it. Still sleeping peacefully, he sighed. Such a human sound from a man who often seemed more than mortal.

Snuggled against him, she fought with herself for much of the night. Berating herself for already being so reliant on him. For wanting him so desperately. For having put herself in this situation in the first place.

But mostly, for being alive when both her parents were dead.

They never should have been separated.

Somehow, Sabine finally fell asleep in his arms. And when she woke? Her husband's hand was exactly where it had been earlier in the night, twisted through her hair and lying directly over her left breast.

She closed her eyes again, trying in vain to ignore her body's response. To do so would be impossible, however, when every last part of her wanted him. Sabine actually opened her mouth to tell him so. To ask for what she wanted. But something she hadn't even known she possessed held her back.

Somehow, she knew it would be more than one night, one act. And Guy had made it clear he was not interested in staying married. Which meant she was not interested in being intimate with him.

A lie, of course. But Sabine had stayed strong. She'd held her tongue and—miracle of miracles— eventually fell back asleep. But not for long.

When the door burst open, Sabine jumped from the bed, taking the coverlet with her.

"You need to dress."

His features were not soft now. In fact, Guy appeared as if he were preparing for battle. She'd not seen him with a hauberk on before. Hadn't even realized he owned one. She had seen many men wearing such shirts of mail, but none of them had looked like this. The effect was devastating to her rapidly ebbing willpower.

Sabine no longer cared if submitting to her husband was the right thing to do. Just then, she would have done so. If not for his next words.

"Lord Burge is here."

His demeanor suddenly took on a new meaning. One that had her scrambling to recover her gown.

"I'll explain later. Meet me outside the chamber as soon as you are ready."

She nodded, her heart thudding incessantly.

He was here. So soon?

Sabine's hands began to tremble as she smoothed out the gown atop the bed. She'd known he would come for her. But that he'd discovered her so soon . . . And he had come himself rather than sending men . .
.

She took a deep breath, cursing the tears in her eyes for betraying her carefully constructed bravado. Why was she so afraid? He had no claim any longer. She was a married woman. But when she thought of him, the messenger of her parent's death . . . the same man who discarded her so easily.

"Sabine."

Guy lay a hand on her arm, his touch as gentle as his soft tone. But it didn't help. She was there again, in Lord Burge's hall, and he was about to tell .
. .

"Sabine?" Guy spun her around.

When she blinked, the tears finally broke loose, dripping silently down her cheeks.

Guy wiped one cheek with his thumb. And then the other.

He breathed in so deeply, she felt compelled to do the same. And then they both did it again, and again. Her heartbeat slowed. Her hands eventually stopped shaking.

"Close your eyes."

She did. Now both hands were on her arms.

"Think of something else, for just a moment. Anything that will make you smile."

Sabine couldn't do it. Not now. Not with Burge just belowstairs. Could he somehow discredit her marriage to Guy?

"Sabine." His tone was both hard and coaxing at the same time.

She'd try . . .

Sabine thought of the river that ran behind their manor. Her mother had always had a terror of water, and so the river had become a special place for Sabine and her father. They'd plunk rocks into the water, one after another, while Mother waved to them from atop the hill.

"Open your eyes."

She did, immediately.

"Control your breathing, control your thoughts . . . and you are prepared for battle."

He dropped his hands.

"'Tis not a battle that awaits us belowstairs," she hesitated. "Or is it?"

Guy sighed. "I do not know. When I entered the hall to fetch us a loaf of bread, I heard whispers of a retinue led by a lord."

"How do you know 'tis Lord Burge?"

"It did not take long for the whispers to gain a name. I came here immediately."

"You feared for me to be alone?"

"Aye."

Though calmer, Sabine was still afraid.

"You are mine now."

Her heart lurched.

"He has no claim on you anymore and will be leaving here with the men who accompanied him. Not"—his eyes narrowed—"with you. Do you understand?"

She nodded.

But then realized . . .

"You are but one man. How many accompany him?"

He cocked his head. "I seem to remember a similar discussion just yesterday. And you'll remember how that ended for a certain sellsword."

She would really have to ask him how a sellsword differed from a mercenary like himself.

"But certainly you would not kill Lord Burge."

Guy reached behind her, his shoulder brushing hers, and picked up her gown. Handing it to her, he said, "For you?"

He turned to leave, but when he reached the door, he turned back to look at her, his expression so serious it sent a shiver down her back.

"I would kill anyone, if necessary. Lord Burge and his men included."

And then he was gone.

CHAPTER 16

By *the blood of Christ.*

After taunting Sabine the previous night, Guy had lain awake for hours attempting to calm his body. Unfortunately, the same training that had allowed him to charge into battle without breaking a sweat had failed him.

Lying next to Sabine, close enough to touch but not touching, had been torturous. So, pretending to be asleep, he'd reached out for her. She'd come to him, nestling close, something that had only inflamed his desire.

By dawn, his need was so urgent, he left her to take a brisk walk. Which was less than relaxing given he immediately heard whispers of Lord Burge's retinue. Now, standing with his back against the wall outside their chamber, he watched for any signs of approach.

Guy thought of his father as he waited. Because, truth be told, he had already known the visiting lord was Burge before he heard the man's name. His father had always been wary of Guy's premonitions, even though he'd witnessed ample evidence that they always came true. Such a thing should be impossible, after all, and Bernard Lavallis had always been the most practical of men. And so, Guy had learned to hide the knowledge he shouldn't have. He'd never told anyone else about the premonitions. Not even Lance and the other men in the order.

If only he'd have one concerning the enigma that was his wife . . .

That very woman appeared, looking as little refreshed as he felt. Guy would have laughed if not for the shadow of Lord Burge.

"Good morn again, my lady."

"Good morn," she murmured back, calmer at least than before. The worry he'd spied in her eyes was still present, however, which made him want to get this matter dealt with immediately. Usually, Sabine took every challenge in turn, always ready to charge on toward the next and take on her next adversary. But this man frightened her.

Which made him want to run a sword through Burge's gut. He'd obviously mistreated her. And was partially responsible for her mother's death. Had he offered her protection, she wouldn't have been with her husband at the time of his demise.

"Is he here?" Sabine asked in a small voice.

Guy took her arm, leading his wife down the stairs.

"I know not."

But he had his answer a moment later. His lady stiffened beside him, and a quick glance at the hall told him all he needed to know—the man who stood near the door had to be Lord Burge.

A handsome older man, he had long, dark-grey hair and a short grey beard. He was dressed for battle, a red and white crest of crossed swords prominent across his chest. The four men around him bore the same crest. Although Burge watched them, he did not move—rather, Guy approached him.

The innkeeper must have sensed the tension because he immediately rushed forward.

"No weapons drawn inside," he stammered. "Do ye hear?"

Burge blocked Guy and Sabine's exit, his eyes drilling into them. Finally, without a word to either of them, he turned and left. The innkeeper's shoulders sank in relief, and Guy winked at the man as they passed.

They still needed lodging and sustenance, after all, when this was over.

Burge's men awaited them as soon as they stepped outside, having formed a semicircle on the path to the stables.

"'Tis Guy Lavallis," one of them said, looking at him. "The mercenary with a sword arm known even in France."

Good. He'd hoped at least one of them would recognize him. Though the man did not look familiar to him at all.

"Good morn, my lord," Sabine said prettily in a tone he was unused to, much more accommodating than usual.

"You are going back," he responded, his tone deep and commanding. This was a man accustomed to issuing commands.

Unfortunately for him, Guy was not at all accustomed to receiving them. But he held his tongue, waiting for Sabine to respond first.

"Nay, my lord. I will not."

He gently let go of her arm, praying she understood the reason. This was her fight, and he didn't wish to take it from her.

That resolution lasted all of a moment. Upon seeing the look of sheer hatred on Burge's face, Guy stepped forward. He couldn't help himself.

"I am Guy Lavallis of Cradney Wrens," he said,

ensuring Burge's man knew he'd identified him correctly. "Lady Sabine's husband," he finished with force. "She will not be going anywhere with you."

Guy momentarily relished the look of shock on their faces. But it did not last long. Burge took a step forward, as did he.

"I don't believe you."

Guy laughed. A response that Burge apparently did not appreciate.

"Visit St. Mary's-upon-Kingsgate on your return home. Speak to Father Wheeland, who will assure you Lady Sabine and I are very much married."

Another step. Burge's men placed their hands on the hilts of their swords. If they chose a fight, Guy would give them one.

"Tell your men to stand down, or this day will be the last they see the sun."

No one liked that particular proclamation. Least of all Burge. He laughed, as if Guy had made a jest, but its tone rang false. Bravado only served a man prepared to fight. And though he had the numbers, Burge had not come here to do battle.

Guy, on the other hand, had done nothing else for his entire life.

"You are one man against five."

He'd have turned to smile at Sabine—hadn't she said much the same thing to him the previous day?—but he didn't dare shift his gaze off Burge's men.

"A fact that matters even less to me than your opinion of our nuptials."

Burge hesitated.

Guy took advantage. Before any of the men could manage a response, he'd withdrawn his sword, the point of which now pricked the bastard's neck.

"At your first movement," he said to the others but with his eyes trained on Burge, "your master dies at my hand."

"Please," Sabine begged from behind. "He's killed one man already on this journey. Leave me be and do as Sir Guy asks. Visit St. Mary's and speak with the priest. I am well and truly married."

Guy smiled at Burge, silently thanking his wife for ensuring the baron knew his rank. Though it mattered little to him, such things could sway a man who cared for titles. And though he had no doubt Burge would kill a fellow knight, especially one who had a sword to his throat, it was a detail that could sway his thinking.

"Drop it," he growled to Burge.

Clearly not pleased, he took a step back as Guy lowered his sword.

The man's shoulders rose and fell, his eyes flashing in anger. But he said nothing. Then, nodding silently to his men, he took another step backward without turning around.

Smart man.

"She owes recompense for the coin paid to the abbey," Burge ground out.

"Nay," Sabine answered. "I owe you nothing."

Burge needed a dignified way out, and Guy gave him one.

"I've instructed Father Wheeland to give you an original manuscript of *Tibericus Psalter*. Keep it, sell it. I care not. Consider it your recompense for Lady Sabine's hasty departure."

Burge's eyes widened. "I shall believe a man such as yourself would be in possession of such a manuscript?"

"Was in possession of it. The book was once given to me by a member of the French court, but aye, you will find it is authentic."

This is your chance, Burge.

Lifting his chin, the baron mumbled something about verifying the truth of his words, but Guy had stopped listening. He turned toward his wife, watching her face to ensure Burge and his men did not act foolishly. By the time he reached her side and took her arm, the men had disappeared into the stables.

Without waiting for them to emerge, Guy escorted Sabine back into the hall. He did ensure they could see the stables from the table they chose. By the time a serving girl brought them a loaf of freshly baked bread, Burge and his men had ridden away.

"I've two questions," Sabine finally asked.

"Only two?"

She made a face that he was beginning to enjoy even if it was meant to discourage his behavior.

"How did you intend to engage with all five men if they attacked you? And why did you give Father Wheeland an original text of one of the most famous French manuscripts in existence?"

He took a bite of bread and followed it with a swig of ale before answering.

"You aren't curious as to how I came to own such a text?"

Her only response was to make that same face.

Guy laughed.

"Very well."

He ignored the appreciative glance of the serving girl, who'd walked by them yet again, and peered outside, just to be certain Burge was indeed gone.

"I could not have hoped to best all four of them if they'd attacked at once, which is why my objective was to ensure they did not do so. And as for the text . . ." He shrugged. "That you would willingly marry a man you obviously hated convinced me such a bribe may be necessary."

Sabine shook her head. "But . . . how did you know . . . how could you have guessed . . . ?"

How indeed.

He waited, but she never finished the thought.

"I have coin to pay you for it."

"Keep your coin," he said between bites. "But we should leave as soon as you are finished, my lady."

She did not look like she would eat, but thankfully, Sabine must have realized it would be many hours before their next meal.

He watched her take a bite of the bread and wondered how such a simple act had never filled him with desire before. But every time she opened her mouth, Guy wondered what it would be like to taste her, to touch her without any clothing between them. Reminded of the miserable night before, he nearly groaned aloud in frustration.

She watched him watching her.

"I do not dislike you."

He bit the inside of his cheek.

"I may have disliked the need to be rescued. And believed you were overly assured of yourself. But I did not hate you. Nor could I ever feel that way now, after everything you have done for me."

His wife did not hate him. What a fine way to begin a marriage, though he kept that thought to himself.

"I do not hate you either, my lady wife."

And when she smiled, Guy's stomach twisted into knots, for the very opposite feeling of hate was beginning to haunt him, as uncontrollable as the premonitions that sometimes intruded on him.

Perhaps she had the right of it. The few moments of pleasure he thought to have with her on this journey would be sweet indeed. But freedom was sweeter still. And he would do well to remember that.

CHAPTER 17

After two more days and nights of torture, Sabine was near ready to break. The tension between her and Guy could be felt every waking moment. Riding throughout the day, he often looked over from his position alongside her. During meals, they spoke of their childhoods, Sabine learning more and more about this man who was nothing like what she'd expected.

Although his mercenary father had raised him, Guy had been on his own for a long, long time. She'd asked why the two had parted ways, but something told her it was a sensitive topic. He told her they'd split over a difference of opinions but did not elaborate.

On the final day of their journey, they stopped midmorning to give their horses a rest. Guy bent down to the stream, and although Sabine could not see what he was doing from her vantage point, she could see his backside quite clearly. When he stood, she turned away quickly, not wanting him to know she'd looked.

Gripping the leather strips of her girdle that hung down from her waist, she twirled them idly through her fingers, thinking of Guy touching her hair in much the same way. It seemed to soothe him, and so she allowed it, but the gesture had become too frequent, too intimate. Sabine was no fool. Each day she and her husband grew closer, which would make their eventual parting more difficult, whether they enjoyed any intimacies or not.

Just the evening before she'd almost begged him to touch her. But his words had stopped her. She'd asked what Guy planned to do next if the order's mission was successful, and though he'd been hesitant to answer, he ultimately admitted he would like to create his own company of mercenaries. To move from place to place, mission to mission, but on his terms.

A life that clearly did not include a wife.

And so she remained silent. Ignored the looks he gave her by the firelight. Ignored her body's response to his not-so-subtle suggestions. They would arrive at Noreham Castle by nightfall, or so he'd said. None too soon for her. Of course, they would not be welcomed as guests.

They would stay in the town, and Guy would privately seek out a meeting with Aceline de Chabannes, the leader of the Bande de Valeur. She would be accompanying him, of course.

"A beautiful piece."

Sabine suppressed the urge to jump. For such a large man, Guy moved with surprising grace and stealth. He stood just behind her, so close Sabine could nearly feel the heat of him.

When he reached around to grab the strips of leather hanging from the belt she'd made, Sabine did not dare move.

"My favorite of your belts that I've seen," he said, fingering the leather, his arm touching her side. She stood completely still lest she accidentally lean into him.

"Mine as well," she admitted.

With no sounds but the distant one of the water trickling through the rocks, Sabine could hear the insistent thud of her own heartbeat.

Nay. Do not. Sabine, 'twill not end well.

Her body responded to the silent plea, and not in the manner she would have liked. With the slightest step backward, she declared her intentions. And Guy noticed. His hand froze, her belt still twined around his fingers.

Still, she could not say the words.

"Sabine?"

The soft caress of her name was too much. About to turn her head, she stopped when Guy pulled her tightly against his chest.

"Do not make me say the words, Guy," she whispered.

One moment her hair lay against her shoulders. The next, she felt its loss as Guy brushed it all to one side. His breath tickled her neck, and she instinctively bent her head, baring her neck to him.

"I am no chivalrous knight," he said into her ear, "who would allow for such a reprieve."

She trembled with the need to feel his touch. But she knew her husband spoke the truth. Although he was far more honorable than he believed himself to be, courtesy had not been bred into him.

"Please?"

Sabine could almost see his smile even though she dared not turn to him. It would be her undoing.

"Nay." His mouth was but a hairsbreadth away from her ear now. "You will need to do better than that."

Her breath came in short bursts as she closed her eyes and imagined what was to come.

"You are a brute."

He did not refute it.

"I offer you"—she swallowed—"me."

And finally, finally his lips brushed the flesh just beneath her ear. So gentle. And yet . . .

They moved lower, down her neck, as he pulled her more tightly against him. He felt as he had in bed. Hard. Unforgiving. Just as his mouth was as it explored every inch of exposed skin. When his hands reached up to cup both breasts, Sabine reached up to grip his wrists, to hold them in place lest he change his mind.

"You taste every bit as sweet as I've imagined."

Sabine did turn her head then, and the look on Guy's face nearly felled her. His expression was softer than she'd ever seen it, and . . . were his eyes glistening? Nay, she must have imagined it. She could hardly think.

"I know not how to proceed," she admitted.

When Guy spun her around, grabbing her face and hauling her back against him, she realized her inexperience didn't matter. He *did* know, and that was enough.

"Open your mouth," he whispered, his voice urgent, and his lips slammed down onto hers. No sooner did she comply than his tongue delved into her mouth, seeking out hers. It took Sabine just a moment to understand, and then their tongues were twining and dancing as the kiss turned ever deeper.

Sabine gave over completely to Guy's ministrations until a clenching gripped her core, much as it had the night he slept nestled against her at the inn.

But this time, the feeling grew stronger and stronger until Sabine wanted, nay needed, more.

She wrapped her hands around his neck, desperately grabbing at his hair. Moving upward, she was finally able to get a good anchor on him. Gripping his hair, she met his every thrust, allowed herself to be pulled deeper and deeper into the moment.

Still holding on to her, Guy pulled back suddenly and looked at her so intently that Sabine was sure he was prepared to say something profound.

"Damn, wife. You can kiss."

Not precisely what she'd been expecting.

"I've had practice," she said as seriously as she could. Waiting a moment, enjoying his scowl, Sabine finally relented and grinned. Realizing she jested with him, Guy growled and kissed her again, so thoroughly that Sabine was sure her lips would be bruised for the effort. Even so, she kissed him harder, urging him to increase his pace.

Every time she'd wondered what it would be like to kiss him, to be close to him, her imagination had failed her. This was so much sweeter.

This time, it was she who broke away. Not because she wanted him to stop, precisely. Just the opposite in fact.

"What you're asking for"—Guy wiped her bottom lip with his thumb—"I'd not give you here." He gestured to the uneven ground beneath them. There was no need for clarification—this particular clearing was not very private. As they approached Noreham, the road had grown wider, more heavily trafficked. Just before they'd stopped, two men, knights by their appearance, had emerged from the very riverbank by which they now stood beside.

"I did not ask for anything," she argued.

"Oh, but you did. And I'd most willingly give it were your safety assured."

He reached up, cupped her head in his hand, and then ran his fingers down through her tresses.

"Tonight."

He kissed her. Hard.

When Guy did pull back, Sabine wasn't even annoyed with his self-assured expression. He looked like a man who'd gotten exactly what he'd wanted from the start. She may be stubborn, but her father had also taught her the uselessness of being spiteful.

Instead, she smiled back. "Then I shall look forward to this evening, husband."

She'd meant it as a promise, but that last word likely reminded them both this was no typical pairing between two people.

It would be a consummation of a marriage.

CHAPTER 18

"**S**ir Guy Lavallis!"

Guy suppressed a groan. He had one mission this eve: to get Sabine out of the camp as quickly as possible. Although Larebridge House attracted fewer unsavory patrons than The Fiddler's Inn, it was not a place he'd care to leave Sabine unattended. As such, he'd been forced to bring his wife to a mercenary camp. Specifically, to the camp of Bande de Valeur, one of the most deadly and badly behaved companies in existence. He knew the fact well. Guy had fought with many, both while he ran with his father and since he'd left him as a young man.

Already Sabine had likely seen more violent and wanton behavior than she'd probably expected to witness in her lifetime. As they led their horses through the field, dark but for the moonlight and several campfires, she'd seen more than enough to warrant the expression she now wore.

A nearly naked camp follower bent before them, picking up a gown that had been tossed from a nearby tent. Wearing nothing other than a thin chemise, the woman yelled back inside, though her words were mumbled.

Guy turned toward the voice that had called to

him, but not before the woman offered him a knowing wink as she strode away.

"Christopher." Guy stuck out his hand. "Well met, lad." When last they'd seen each other, Christopher had been more boy than man, but he'd grown several inches and his cheeks had narrowed. He'd always had a fondness for the lad.

"No longer that," his former companion said, shaking his hand vigorously. He grinned as if Guy were his long-lost brother.

"Aye, you've grown into a man."

"I'd not expected to see you again." Christopher shifted his gaze to Sabine, the look he gave her much too appreciative. Nay, no longer a boy.

"Meet my wife, Lady Sabine."

Christopher bowed prettily.

"This," he said to his wife, "is Christopher Logue. Son of a right old bastard who nearly had me killed in Arbois."

"A pleasure," Sabine murmured.

Though he was as pleased to see Christopher as anyone in this camp, he needed to get Sabine away from these men. And quickly.

"Where is he?" Guy asked.

Christopher nodded to the tent Guy had assumed was the leader's, being both larger than the others and at the very center of camp.

"Shall I take your horses?"

Guy handed him the reins. "Gladly, though not far, if it pleases you. This will not be an extended visit."

His purpose this night was simply to alert de Chabannes of his presence and set a meeting for their negotiations. It would take days, if not weeks, for any outcome, much less a favorable one. Guy knew the mercenary company's leader as well as anyone. And did not expect him to capitulate easily.

But he would capitulate. Eventually.

"Many thanks." He took Sabine's hand. Squeezing it, he leaned toward her to whisper as they walked toward de Chabannes's tent.

"Say little."

She pulled back.

"I do not ask it of you out of a desire to silence you. But to protect you. De Chabannes is cunning and will attempt to use any information you give him."

Sabine did not appear pleased by the prospect, but neither did she refute him.

Just before they entered, he whispered again.

"I will ensure you are rewarded for your efforts later."

His wife's gasp was the last thing he heard before entering the tent.

❧

SABINE HADN'T EXPECTED THE MAN GUY DESCRIBED as a ruthless bastard to bound up from his seat to hug her husband.

Though she understood some of his words, it had been years since Sabine had studied French. When her tutor took ill, her mother had completed Sabine's studies, and though she herself had been fluent in the language, as most noblewomen were, it was not an area of study Sabine enjoyed. And, as her father had said many, many times, her mother had been too indulgent of Sabine's whims.

The mercenary leader also spoke quickly, though Guy seemed to have no difficulty understanding him.

Since she could not hope to understand what they were saying, Sabine watched the two. She was struck most by Guy's easy manner, as if he'd not spent much of the day warning Sabine about this very man. Not that she could think of much besides that kiss, which she knew had affected them equally. Each time she looked at Guy, his expression told the tale. One of desire, of longing, and of anticipation.

"*Mieux vaut être seul que mal accompagné,*" de Chabannes spat.

That she understood, mostly. Guy had asked why he was alone in the tent, something unusual for him, and he'd responded that he'd prefer to be alone than in bad company.

Guy gestured back to her. "Lady Sabine, daughter of Robert de Stuteville, lord of Cottingham." He paused. "My wife."

The mercenary seemed as shocked as Christopher had been. Apparently the idea of Guy having a wife was a startling one. He recovered quickly, though, and bowed more deeply than was her due. Sabine had never met a Frenchman who would risk offense by failing to offer a proper greeting.

"The honor is mine," he said, standing. Now that she had a better look at him, she realized he was quite a bit younger than she'd expected. His face bore a similar scar to Conrad's, although in a different location. It was a hard face, accustomed to both battle and the elements. Though not clean-shaven, like Guy, neither did he have a beard.

De Chabannes filled two goblets with wine, which he then gave to Sabine and Guy, gesturing for them to sit across from him on a wide stool. His tent accommodated four such structures and was obviously the center of the company's activities. It struck her that it would take some effort to transport its contents, especially across the channel.

This was no small favor Guy planned to ask for.

"What brings you, along with your wife, to my humble tent?"

"I'm here to negotiate on behalf of the Order of

the Broken Blade." The change in Guy's demeanor caught her off guard. His easy grins and teasing jests had slipped away, leaving the very serious, very driven man she remembered from that first night at the abbey.

De Chabannes sat up a bit straighter.

"An order," Guy continued, "formed to force the English king to heed the pleas of his barons."

And there it was. Treason against the king.

"What, precisely, do you hope to negotiate with your visit?"

Guy placed his wine goblet on the bench beside him.

"Your return to France."

De Chabannes took a long sip of wine as he stared at her husband, his eyes revealing nothing. "I've not heard of this order," he said at last.

"You will."

It was as if a gentle wind had run along her body, riffling her hair.

"The hour is late, and we've traveled far," Guy said. "My intent this eve was simply to alert you to our presence in the village, as I know you'd have learned of it by morn. And to arrange another meeting between us."

The leader looked at her. Sabine said nothing.

"We have been paid handsomely to sit in these tents and wait," de Chabannes remarked simply.

He did not have to explain what his men waited for. All three of them knew King John would rather unleash a foreign army of mercenaries on his people than listen to their concerns. Or so it seemed at present.

"I am aware."

Sabine took a sip of her wine, trying to appreciate its fine quality.

"Who's paying you?" De Chabannes's jaw flexed. A fair question to ask a mercenary.

"No one."

Sabine did not understand the look that passed between the men, but she did know it held some significance. She would ask Guy about it later. For now, she fought her very nature and said nothing, continuing to sip the wine she'd nearly finished.

De Chabannes stood abruptly. Sabine held her breath as he walked toward them, but at the last moment he reached for the pitcher and held out his hand for her silver goblet. Somehow, he knew she'd already finished her wine. After refreshing both her drink and his own, de Chabannes sat back down.

Guy had not so much as sipped his wine.

"This order?"

Guy did not hesitate. "The Earl of Licheford. The chief of Clan Kennaugh and Earl of Dromsley, and Sir Lancelin Wayland of Marwood, now lord of Tuleen."

He had just named all three men as traitors, but Sabine supposed it was necessary to gain de Chabannes's trust before he would be swayed. Still, the boldness of his speech terrified her. One whisper in the wrong ear, and all four of them could be branded as traitors to the crown.

And me as well.

She took another long sip of wine.

De Chabannes nodded, more to himself than as a gesture to Guy. After a few moments, he stood again.

"It seems we have much to discuss."

Guy stood as well and reached for her goblet. Taking it, he handed both to de Chabannes and offered Sabine his hand. She took it gladly, grateful for its strength. When Guy laced his fingers through hers, a calm settled within her for the first time since they entered the tent.

"Aye, we do. Sabine and I will be staying at Larebridge House."

"I will send for you."

Guy nodded. With a few parting words, Sabine found herself walking away from the tent, still holding her husband's hand. She tried to imagine him as one of the men still milling about camp, despite the late hour. So many seemed to know of him, and his deeds, but to her, Guy was more than the greatest swordsman in all of England.

He was her husband.

"You did well," he said at last as they walked toward their horses.

She made a sound in her throat.

"By not speaking? That was hardly my best performance."

Guy stopped and looked at her with admiration.

"A performance nonetheless, for I know remaining silent went against your very nature."

Indeed, it did.

"Thankfully, I requested the only room at the inn set apart from the others."

"I do not understand."

But his wicked grin explained his meaning even before he spoke. "You're welcome to make as much noise as you'd like when we return. 'Tis my turn to perform for you."

CHAPTER 19

There were many things Guy lacked, but coin was not one of them. He'd been trained at the French court by one of the most renowned swordsmen in his mother's country, experience that had helped him win almost every tournament he entered.

But never had he been so pleased with his success as he was at this moment. Sabine had shrieked with pleasure upon seeing the room he'd secured for them, complete with a steaming hot bath that sat in the middle of it. He'd left her there to enjoy it, heading downstairs to the hall to enjoy an ale while he waited.

The additional coin had also offered them some much-needed privacy—a wooden bridge connected their second-floor room to the rest of the inn. He'd learned about this space on his last visit. The owner of Larebridge House, a man as large as Terric but with the stomach size to match the girth of his wide shoulders, had taken a liking to him.

"Ya remind me of my son," the man had told him. The two had gotten drunk together, a rarity for Guy. But then the innkeeper had told him the full story of his lost family, and he'd quickly sobered. The man had woken up one morning to find his wife had left him, taking his son.

The story had reminded Guy too much of his own mother. She'd left overnight too, only she hadn't taken him with her. His last memory was of her smiling down at him. But apparently she loved France far more than she loved him, for she'd returned to her home country without him. Without saying goodbye either.

Guy silently reminded himself to thank the innkeeper again for the use of the "bridge room." Although he was grateful for the privacy it afforded, it would serve another purpose—he could see the bridge from where he sat in the inn's small hall. Which meant he could ensure no one disturbed his wife. He was certain Burge was no longer a concern, but that did not mean Sabine was ever completely safe unless Guy was near.

And when you leave her?

Pushing aside the thought, and his nearly empty mug of ale, Guy made his way up the stairs and across the creaky bridge he had been staring at just moments earlier. Built for the king's visit more than twenty years earlier, the room was now reserved for important nobles and, tonight, a mercenary and his wife.

Wife.

Guy could not remember anticipating an evening as much as this one. It had been a long day of travel, followed by the tense visit with de Chabannes, which had gone precisely how he'd expected.

But after that kiss? Sleep could wait.

He could not.

Guy had thought he'd given her plenty of time to bathe, but when he opened the door, he nearly stumbled. The size of four regular rooms at the inn, this vast space would look completely at home in

Licheford or Dromsley Castle. Even so, he had a clear view of Sabine scrambling to cover herself inside the large wooden tub he'd commissioned earlier.

She ducked into the water, dipping so far down only her head showed, her wet hair glistening in the light from the candles arranged around her and the wall torches flickering in their sconces. The tub was so large a footstool lay next to it, but it was neither the stool nor the drying cloth draped over a nearby table Guy focused on as he walked toward his wife.

"I thought you'd have finished by now."

Though she'd covered her breasts, Guy could clearly see a darkness within the water that beckoned him. If the King of England himself attempted to beat down the door, Guy would not allow him entry. Nothing would keep him from her.

He'd never wanted anyone or anything more in his life.

Removing his clothing, piece by piece, he thought of the ride here. More torturous than being captured by a bloodthirsty earl's retinue or having his arm sliced nearly in two—both of which Guy had experienced.

More than once he'd considered dismounting and tossing caution aside to take Sabine right alongside the road. From the moment she had acquiesced, he could think of nothing other than slipping into her, claiming her as his.

A dangerous thought.

"What are you about?"

He didn't answer. She would guess in due time.

"There's no need to cover yourself, Sabine. I am your husband."

"For a time." She did not remove her hands.

Again, he didn't answer.

Instead, Guy stayed his hand on the waist of his

braies, the last vestige of any sort of modesty between them.

"Have you changed your mind, then?"

Guy willed her to say no, although he would of course honor her decision had she changed her mind.

"I have not."

Sabine had once accused him of being many people—she'd told him that she struggled to understand which Guy Lavallis was the "real" one. He often felt the same about his wife. Fearless at times. Modest at others. Which Sabine would greet him now?

Guy would soon find out.

"Oh my!" she said as he slipped free of his braies.

He could do with such a reaction. Smiling, Guy moved to the tub.

"Surely you don't mean to . . ."

She sat up to accommodate him, knowing exactly what he meant to do. But he mistook her meaning apurpose.

"To make you as wet as the water in which we sit?"

He straddled her legs, settling in quite nicely. The tub made for a tight fit, but it held both of them.

"To make love to you until the sun rises? Aye, I mean to do both and more."

With her hair wet around her shoulders, a drip of water on her nose, she was like a water nymph, something so beautiful it belonged in another world.

I do not deserve her.

His extremely hard cock brushed against her stomach, and Guy knew it would take tremendous effort not to enter her too soon. Clenching his jaw, he gripped both sides of the tub.

When two delicate hands tentatively lay on his back, Guy sucked in a breath.

Slow and easy.

He leaned down and kissed her. It was so different from their earlier kiss, the gentleness of it seeming to startle her. Coaxing her mouth open, his tongue stroked and teased until he grew even harder, the need to be inside her so very strong.

Slanting his mouth across hers, Guy deepened their kiss, allowing his chest to press against hers. He wanted to feel the two mounds with his hands and cursed the decision to make love to her in the tub.

He'd not wanted to wait, but neither could he fully indulge as he would later when they lay in the bed. For now, he relished the feel of her lips against his. Her hands against his neck and head, pressing him more firmly against her.

Shifting all of his weight to one hand, Guy reached under the water, the small splash tossing droplets of water over them. Finding the underwater treasure, Guy slipped his fingers inside, making Sabine flinch.

Lifting his head, he reassured her with a smile. One that promised she'd be well taken care of, in every way.

"Open a bit for me if you can."

She did, and he drove his fingers in deeper. When Sabine dropped her mouth open in surprise, he decided he would watch her face, her every expression, as she came in his hands.

Instead of kissing her, Guy offered words instead.

"This"—he used his thumb to instruct her—"is your most sensitive place. You see, if I rub it like so . . ."

She pushed her hips into his fingers.

"The need for release will make you want more. Deeper"—his movements matched his words—"faster." Water splashed all around them. "Until your body screams in protest from building to such a crescendo but not being allowed to uncoil."

CHAPTER 20

Sabine could not think. She could do nothing but allow herself to be carried from the tub like a babe. When she gingerly set her feet down on the floor, she was unsure of her ability to stand.

He was there almost immediately with the drying cloth, but rather than give it to her, he began gliding it down her body, across her stomach. When he knelt down to dry her legs, Sabine finally began to regain some semblance of steady breathing.

But it didn't last long.

"I'm unsure I need to be dried there."

When he looked up, Sabine could see his face against the backdrop of his muscled shoulders. The heady combination, along with the current location of his hands, nearly made her knees buckle again. She held on for support as Guy chuckled.

"Unsteady?"

He seemed pleased by the fact.

Sabine would have responded, but Guy stood then. She watched as he dried himself.

"So many scars," she murmured, not daring to look down.

Guy tossed the cloth to the side. Although he wasn't grinning, she could tell he held back a smile.

"You laugh at me," she said, wanting to fetch the cloth and cover herself.

"Nay," he said, unmoving. "Though I intend to shed you of a lifetime of modesty."

He broke eye contact to slowly lower his gaze down her body. As he did, Sabine could think only of hiding herself, but when she moved to do so, Guy shook his head. For reasons beyond her understanding, she acquiesced.

"Your turn."

Sabine had never felt so exposed. She complied, though, and did as he had done. Arms of a warrior, a flat stomach with at least two scars that she could see to match those on his shoulders. Four? Nay, five. Mayhap he should wear armor more often.

And then she finally looked lower. Hard and thick, his manhood was as she remembered from the brief glance she'd taken when he entered the bath. So very different from her.

When he closed the distance between them, Sabine gave in to the need to touch him. She wrapped her palm around him, and Guy guided her hand into stroking him up and down. Closing his eyes, her husband let go as she continued on her own. When he bit the inside of his cheek, Sabine actually smiled. Then she remembered how he'd pleasured her. Slowly, at first, and then faster and faster. So she did the same, knowing by his expression her aim had found its mark.

His eyes flew open as his hand covered hers once again, stopping the movements.

"You learn quickly."

With that, he hauled her against his chest, kissing her with such force it actually startled her for the briefest of moments. But then, all modesty set aside for the moment, Sabine allowed herself to revel in the intense pleasure her husband provided. As he moved them toward the bed, his hands were everywhere at once. But there was one place she wanted them most, so she grabbed his hand and moved it.

Guy simultaneously lifted her onto the bed and complied with her not-so-subtle ministrations.

"You've only but to ask," he breathed into her ear, his fingers complying with her silent plea. "If you want my fingers inside you, tell me. If you want my cock inside instead, I'm happy to comply."

Guy spread her legs apart with his free hand.

"If you wish for me to kiss you there"—he bit gently on her earlobe—"say it and my tongue will do so gladly."

Sabine had two thoughts simultaneously. First, the building of pleasure inside her was about to explode as it had done before. And second . . . his tongue . . . *there*?

"Guy . . ." She knew not what she intended to say.

Suddenly, his hand was gone. Lifting himself above her, Guy positioned himself to enter her but did not move. Instead he watched her, waiting. For a signal? For her to say something?

"You'll be a maiden no longer," he said, the strain of holding back evident on his face. "But I will ensure a babe will not swell your belly."

Her heart lurched at that. Surely she would go to hell for such an act, for preventing life from growing inside her. Selfishly, she wanted to be with her husband anyway. They could not have a future together, but they could have this.

Nodding, Sabine watched as he guided himself easily inside. It felt . . . neither good nor bad. Though she kept the sentiment to herself.

"It will hurt."

She knew the truth of his words—her mother had

warned her—but the stinging that came a moment later when he thrust inside tore a sound from deep within her throat.

Grasping his shoulders, she pushed him away, but Guy did not move.

"Hold still."

Even as he said it, the intense pain began to abate.

"I'm unsure about this," Sabine admitted.

"I am not."

He moved then, so very slowly she could barely feel the movement. This time, there was no pain. He kissed her, making Sabine forget everything but his lips slanting over hers. She thought of the night they met, when he'd held her wrists above her, alluding to this very moment.

Never had she thought they would be in this position in such a short time. That she'd have willing given herself to the arrogant mercenary. And never had she imagined the feelings he would awaken inside her. When Guy moved more quickly, she grasped the back of his head for some stability.

As if any could be found. She was falling deeper and deeper, her lips tearing away to allow for the moan she'd never heard herself make before. The sound seemed to stir something in him, because Guy thrust even deeper that time, reaching his hand between them and nearly causing her to leap from the bed.

Except she wanted very much to be here. With him.

She grabbed his hair, pushed up her hips, and called out his name.

Sabine's buttocks clenched together as the same tension from before unfurled in her body. Her shoulders shook with the effort, and just as she became aware of herself again, Guy pulled away with such a primeval grunt of pleasure that she nearly cried out at the loss.

Only when she was able to breathe again did she notice he'd propped himself above her. Looking down at the drying cloth next to them on the bed, she grappled to understand. When had he even moved that to the bed?

She looked up, waiting for an explanation.

"If I came inside you, you could grow heavy with child."

Ah. Of course.

"It seems wrong, somehow."

And she didn't mean that preventing such a thing was condemned by God. This had nothing to do with the Church at all.

Guy swallowed. "'Tis not natural to pull away. Every part of me wished not to do so."

Sabine took a deep, steadying breath. "*Every* part?"

She waited for his answer. They both knew what she was asking.

Finally, he shook his head ever so slightly. "Nay, not every one."

Sabine closed her eyes, pretending his words did not feel as if he'd ripped her heart from her chest. This is what she had asked for. It was what she'd wanted.

Wasn't it?

CHAPTER 21

He wanted to wake her.

But he also wanted for Sabine to remain sleeping. For when she woke, he wasn't sure what he'd say to her. That last eve had shaken him more than he wished to admit? That he'd considered staying inside her for the duration? That, for one wild moment, he'd thought he might be glad for it if she *did* swell with child?

Nay, he could not say any of that. Even as he pulled her closer to him, Guy admitted to himself that such sentiments were dangerous. He had never considered marriage before. A true marriage. But a man's plans could change—he knew that better than anyone—nay, that was not the reason he should push Sabine away.

He knew he hardly deserved such a woman. He was a bastard, if not in the true sense of the word. He'd not lied about that. Guy had fought for good men, but he'd fought for bad ones too. That he was beyond redemption was a fact he'd learned to live with, despite his friend Terric's insistence that he judged himself too harshly. And yet, the knowledge that she was much too good for him was not enough to keep him from her.

He was ruthless, mayhap heartless at times, but he would be neither of those with her. Nay, the reason they'd do best to part soon, before either of them fell any deeper, was because this life he led was a hard one. An itinerant one. Staying in one place too long had always unsettled him, and for as long as he could remember, he'd dreamed of leading his own company of mercenaries.

Eventually Sabine would grow weary of life on the road. Perhaps, like his mother, she'd leave one night. Guy could not survive another loss like that. Neither would he bring a child into the world to experience the anguish he'd felt the morning he'd awoken to find his mother had returned to France without him.

When Sabine shifted against him, Guy moved away. Though it was still dark, he swung his legs off the side of the bed.

"The sun has not even risen."

She sounded sleepy still. And content.

"Stay abed." He didn't turn around. "'Tis early, as you said."

When her hand touched his bare back, Guy flinched. He closed his eyes and imagined grasping it in his own. Holding it above her head and then finding the other, keeping her captive beneath him all morning. Nay, all day. Awaiting word from de Chabannes while buried deep inside her.

But she had the right of it. Intimacy between them was serving only to complicate an already complicated relationship.

"I did not sleep well," he said truthfully, standing.

Guy dressed without glancing her way. If he knew de Chabannes, his wait would not be a long one. They were here, in Noreham's village, for a purpose. It would serve him well to remember that.

He could hear her lying back down.

As he was about to pull a tunic over his head, Guy glimpsed the belt Sabine had crafted.

"Shall we visit the village today? Perhaps there is a girdler nearby." He picked up the piece. "This really is a fine girdle."

Although he'd intended to wait for her in the hall, Guy changed his mind and sat on the bed.

"How do you do this?"

"I simply stitched together two narrow bands and finished it with silk fringe. My mother taught me how."

He paused. "You miss them very much. Your parents."

"Aye." Sabine sat up then, and Guy tried not to peer down the wide opening in the front of her shift. "I often wonder what they'd think of the choices I've made thus far."

Though she shrugged, Guy sensed there was nothing casual about her words.

"Though my upbringing was not as conventional as most, my father would have seen me married long ago. Thankfully, my mother had much to say on the matter and believed in my abilities."

"Can you not be both capable and married?"

He could tell from her expression she doubted such a thing were possible.

"Wouldn't your mother be an example of someone who did both?"

"Aye. And I understand your meaning. My father was not a typical man. But for all of his protectiveness, I was left alone and sold to an abbey. So I would sooner depend on myself than rely on others."

Others. Meaning him.

Guy stood. "I would imagine he was anything but typical."

Strapping his sword to his belt, Guy refrained from clarifying his statement. The parents of extraordinary children often had much to recommend them too, and Sabine was nothing if not extraordinary. But he left that part unsaid.

"I will be just below. Join me when you're willing."

With that, he left, lest he say too much to his wife.

※

SABINE WOKE FOR A SECOND TIME. WHEN SHE opened the shutters, the sunlight beamed through them, although she could tell it had newly risen.

When the door opened, she'd just finished dressing in her one and only gown. At home, she had worn a different one each day. And although not elaborate, they'd been made from the finest fabric and adorned with belts she made herself, or ones given to her by her mother. With such a beautiful piece draped across her hips, Sabine never desired to wear additional baubles.

"We leave immediately for Noreham Castle."

Guy had returned looking every bit the part of a dangerous, handsome mercenary. The look on his face confirmed that trouble was afoot.

"Noreham Castle? You wish to visit the very lord who is hosting the company of mercenaries you hope to send home. Is that wise?"

Guy did not leave his position near the door.

"Nay, likely not. But neither do I wish for you to remain here, unprotected."

"I meant is it wise for you?"

Guy seemed to consider the question for a moment. "Again, likely not. But de Chabannes sent word that we are to join him at the midday meal as guests of the baron."

No mention of the previous night. Or of the blood on the sheets that she'd rolled up and left at the foot of the bed. Or of anything other than their next venture.

If he could play that game, so could she.

"Do you find it unusual, such a request?"

Guy shut the door finally, making her jump at the sound.

"I do. Though we've no choice but to accept."

She opened her mouth to ask a question, but Guy answered her before she could ask it.

"But nay, I do not believe de Chabannes has told the lord of our betrayal. I suspect he means to remind me that he can do so at any time. A fact I don't believe we'll be forgetting."

Neither of them said anything after that. Guy looked as if he wanted to speak, but when he remained silent, Sabine did the same. It was only when she finished preparing and strode toward him that Guy reacted at all. He opened the door, as if eager to escape, and stood far away from it to let her pass.

He clearly regretted his actions from the night before. Sabine, however, did not. She tried to ignore the jolt of pain his reaction caused.

They rode through the village in silence, Sabine taking in each building as they passed. A tannery with a well alongside it. The mill and a blacksmith's shop along a small stream that followed the path they were travelling. They passed through fields, too, some planted and others fallowed. A handsome, though small, chapel marked the end of the dirt road on which they traveled. She'd not spied that earlier. Indeed, she'd thought there were none in the vicinity. Though a large demesne separated them from the castle, the fertile green land untouched, she could see it easily.

As they approached the castle, Sabine alternated between worrying over what to expect from the lord of Noreham and what to expect from her husband.

It was the former that demanded her attention at present. It was less confusing, for one, and for another, it was more likely to get her killed in the immediate future. Two of the baron's men rode up to them, the same crest on their tunics as was flying high overhead above the main gate. Overly large, its stone arch supported two of the largest wooden doors Sabine had ever seen in her life. She supposed without a drawbridge, any approach would be met with the same, but it unnerved her nonetheless.

"Sir Guy Lavallis?"

"Aye." Guy rode up to them. "And my wife, Lady Sabine, if it pleases you."

The same man who'd greeted them grunted in response, turning back toward the gate. They followed, a loud crack of thunder hastening their journey toward the inner bailey, where servants and men-at-arms already hurried to take cover. Sabine flinched as another crack of thunder filled the air, this one louder than the first. Dismounting quickly and handing their reins to a stable boy, she and Guy followed the men who'd greeted them into the main keep. When they stopped in front of a pair of double doors, she wasn't expecting another courtyard, but a wide open space greeted them. Unfortunately, the clouds unloosed a deluge on them, so they hurried to and through another door, Sabine tripping on the raised floor beyond the doorstep.

Guy caught her before she stumbled forward. As his arms encircled her, Sabine fought the urge to grip him and not let go. Though her footing was steady, her heart beat wildly in her chest, and the great hall and its occupants fell away as she stared into her husband's hungry eyes.

The spell was broken by a voice from the other end of the hall.

"Lavallis!"

De Chabannes stood at the foot of the head table in the great hall, as if he'd just arrived himself. She slipped her hand through his arm as they approached the lord of Noreham, who sat behind a massive head table. There was no lady that Sabine could see, just a large empty wooden chair next to him.

He was young, this lord who championed a ruthless king. And handsome, though the knowledge of his complicity made him ugly to her. Some would call him loyal, but not Sabine. To her, anyone who could close their eyes to King John's special kind of cruelty was as much a part of the problem as the ambitious leader himself. It had taken just one story, of the Baroness of Elmwood, to sway Sabine to the rebels' cause. The widow had been imprisoned in the Tower simply for claiming her husband's title for her son, a common practice. Unfortunately, John wanted it back and the baroness had to choose between her son's inheritance and her life.

This was a cause her father had taken up before most others, including the order.

Relying on her training, Sabine smiled at the lord of Noreham, nodding her acknowledgment of the mercenary leader as well. She said nothing as the men exchanged polite greetings and introductions.

The baron nodded to her. "Lavallis is indeed a lucky man to have such a lady as his wife."

She simply smiled, thinking little of the remark, until she noticed Guy's dark look. For a very brief moment, Guy looked like he intended to throttle Noreham, but the look disappeared as quickly as it had come, replaced by an expression of forced good cheer.

With the introductions no longer demanding her attention, Sabine looked upward, admiring the vaulted ceiling. By now the hall was filled with retainers and guests. No fewer than fifty people sat around them, the white table linens in stark contrast to a darkness in the hall no amount of candles could illuminate. Perhaps it felt so cold because so few females were in attendance. Or maybe it was the abundance of weapons that graced the walls around them.

When they sat at a table some distance from Noreham's, she felt marginally more comfortable, except that de Chabannes and his men were seated opposite them.

"You want to know why I asked you here," de Chabannes began, a mouthful of stew still making its way down his throat.

"I want to know who did the asking," Guy responded. Though the other men at their table were obviously members of Bande de Valeur, they sat close to other tables filled with Noreham's men. So Sabine was surprised when de Chabannes answered so openly.

"I told the baron of your arrival, and it was he who requested your presence."

She refrained from looking at Guy, knowing it would be hard to keep any emotion from her expression. Instead, she stared down into her bowl, concerned. Neither piece of news boded well for their mission here.

Guy surprised her. "I should have expected you to do so," he said, his tone serious.

The look that passed between the two of them did not seem like a communication between a former master and his man. This was a look of deadly understanding between equals. Except one was at a decided disadvantage. Sitting in the hall of a powerful baron loyal to the king, the table and hall filled with men who would gladly destroy Guy and his friends and those who'd joined their cause . . . aye, it was likely a position de Chabannes had intentionally maneuvered.

The meal passed without incident. When

CHAPTER 22

Guy was essentially a prisoner here, but it bothered him more that Sabine was in the same position. Still, the thought of leaving her at the inn had been unacceptable.

Although he'd never admit it, Guy should have listened to Conrad and taken some of his friend's men with him. He had dismissed the idea as quickly as he had the earl's many suggestions that Guy remain in his service. Terric had suggested the same throughout the years, but Guy had always declined.

He did better on his own.

But you're not alone now. You have a wife.

As they sat in the baron's solar, he was reminded of how vulnerable that made him. He was glad neither Noreham nor de Chabannes commented on her presence even though it was highly unusual. But without Sabine, he'd have thought nothing of attempting to escape this place should Noreham actually retain him. At worst, he'd pay for bad judgement in a traitor's jail, perhaps even with his life. But now there was a fate much worse than that.

The possibility that Sabine might be subjected to the same.

He tried not to glare at de Chabannes for having

put him in this situation. The man was loyal to one person. Himself. Even so, Guy still did not believe he would have told Noreham of the order's hope to send the company back to France.

"You worked with him once?" Noreham asked, sitting back in his chair. The baron was known to control the nearby port, which was sometimes used for the king's transport. He'd assumed the man would be much older, but Noreham was close to him in age. Not yet thirty.

Aside from the few facts Conrad had given him, Guy knew little else about this man, including how he'd inherited such a stronghold so young.

"I did," he said, "many years ago."

"You must have been quite young?"

Guy could say the same but did not.

"Aye. My father joined Bande de Valeur when I was just ten and two."

"He is a mercenary as well?"

"Aye."

He was giving no more information than he received.

"So how did you come to be under Lord Noreham's protection?" he asked de Chabannes.

The air, so thick with hidden loyalties and unspoken accusations, shifted slightly. Somehow, it had become even denser.

"I believe Lord Noreham would be better able to answer your question."

Unfortunately, the lord in question was looking at his wife. It was not the first time that eve he'd done so, though Guy very much wished it would be the last. He could not discern if it was interest or something more sinister, but the nuance hardly mattered.

He wanted to pummel the man, and if the baron persisted in his staring, he just might. After all, it was de Chabannes he needed to persuade, not this supporter of a corrupt king.

"I had the land," Noreham said, his eyes darting between Guy and Sabine.

"And did our king give you a reason for their arrival?"

He may have gone too far. By the expressions of every single person in the room, including his wife, his companions certainly seemed to believe so.

But Guy was here to turn the tide of a potential war, and his side would lose if Bande de Valeur stayed. He needed answers.

"He said," Noreham said carefully, "they were here to ensure peace."

Or just the opposite.

Guy decided to push further.

"And you believed him?"

Surprisingly, though de Chabannes gasped, which was very unlike the man, Noreham did not flinch. Instead, he turned to Sabine.

"What would you have done, my lady?"

She cocked her head to the side. "I apologize, my lord. I am not as well-versed in politics as my husband."

Guy nearly choked on the wine he had just sipped. She'd said it without a hint of a smile . . . God, the woman was good.

In many ways.

Of course, the memory of her sprawled beneath him in bed was unlikely to help him think a way out of the very tricky situation in which they were currently embroiled.

"Is that so?"

Her eyes did not betray her, but the slight stiffening of her shoulders did. Whether he was the only one to notice or not, they would soon find out. But to him, it was clear.

Sabine lied as ably as every man in this chamber.

"'Tis so, my lord. Though if you need assistance in other areas, I may be of service."

When Noreham's brows lifted at that, Guy nearly leapt up from his seat. Sabine must have sensed both reactions, as she rushed to explain.

"I noticed the tapestries in your hall, though very beautiful, could use a cleaning. My mother discovered a method that does not require removing them from the wall."

Noreham smiled then, a seductive smile that made Guy grit his teeth.

"Permit me to speak to your steward," Sabine cut in quickly, standing.

Guy tried to tell her to sit back down with his eyes, but she did not take his meaning. Or perhaps she simply ignored him. A more likely scenario. Either way, she left them with Noreham's assurance his man was standing just outside the chamber.

If they made it out of this keep alive, Guy would kill her for putting her life in danger.

Because the baron's expression left him with no doubt—this was no friendly discussion between men. It was a deadly game, and for the moment, he and Sabine were at a disadvantage. But that was about to change.

CHAPTER 23

They didn't speak on the ride back. Sabine wanted to know everything that had been said in her absence, but Guy insisted it was a poor idea for them to start yelling back and forth as they rode through Lord Noreham's lands. She knew the true reason: he was furious she'd left his "care."

The moment they entered their room, the bed freshly made and a bowl of rosewater awaiting their arrival, Sabine spun on him.

"You look at me as if I am to blame for de Chabannes's wretchedness."

"Nay." Guy walked around her as he removed his sword and belt, placing both near the bed. "Only for separating yourself from me and putting yourself in danger."

"He was suspicious."

"With good reason."

"And I suspect he may have known my father."

"A fair assumption given the way he looked at you."

Removing his padded gambeson and boots, Guy did not even turn around to look at her.

Sabine angrily took off her own shoes and stockings, ignoring him just as assuredly.

"You are not to blame for that," he said at last. "But I wasn't pleased by my inability to stop him from staring at you so."

"What would you have done had we not been in danger of being held there as traitors?"

Sabine was not sure how she felt about Guy's jealousy, but she was most definitely curious to know how far he would have taken it.

"I'd have asked for him to join me in the training yard, where I would have earned my reputation as the greatest swordsman in England."

Tossing her hose aside, Sabine planted her hands on her hips.

"'Tis quite a boast."

Guy chose that moment to lift his linen shirt above his head. Clad in nothing but trewes, he was nothing short of magnificent.

"And a true one, as Noreham would have learned."

A feeling of warmth coursed through her. Dismissing it, she asked, "What happened after I left?"

Guy shrugged. "I made mention of Carcassonne, reminding de Chabannes that perhaps he should have more loyalty for a fellow mercenary than a king's man."

"Carcassonne?"

"Where I saved his life."

"You . . . you saved de Chabannes's life? And did not think to mention it to me?"

Guy frowned. "There's much we haven't spoken of, Sabine."

"Such as?"

He took a step toward her.

"How Lance and I met Conrad and Terric at the Tournament of the North. We came upon one of the king's men poised to rape Terric's sister. Just children, or barely beyond it, we overpowered him together. We killed the man and dumped his body in the river."

Sabine froze.

"I've not told you about all the nights I cried myself to sleep wondering how a mother could simply walk away from her only child. Or how I somehow felt she might do so, a fact that terrified my father. Or the ones I lay awake wondering how a man who wants nothing more than to be alone craves the company of a woman already pledged to him."

Sabine wanted both to weep at his loss and smile at his admission.

"I've not made mention"—he closed the distance between them—"how, for the first time in my life, I became angered by the mere suggestion that another man might want the woman I care for."

Her chest heaved as it rose and fell.

"Nor have I admitted that I want this mission to succeed as much for you and your parents' sacrifice as for my brothers in the order."

"But most of all, I regret not having mentioned before this moment that not spilling my seed into you last eve was the most difficult thing I've ever done. And not something I ever wish to repeat."

They stood there staring at each other, neither making a move. All she had to do was reach for him. Admit to herself that needing Guy was not the same as needing her parents. When they'd been taken from her, she'd been lost. As lost as she would be if Guy walked away from their marriage.

Just say it. Ask him. Find out this very moment if he still plans to leave you when his business with de Chabannes is all over.

Nay, you need only say three simple words.

I love you.

All she needed to do was speak the words aloud.

CHAPTER 24

S abine said nothing.

Guy's heart throbbed in his chest, but it didn't matter, he wanted her anyway. Even though he'd just admitted more to her than he should have, more than he'd consciously realized himself. Tomorrow would be soon enough to consider what it all meant.

Right now he wanted only to show her pleasure, this woman who was his wife. Who had blackmailed him. Who had escaped from a destiny that would have crushed most people. Who'd been betrayed by the overlord her parents had reluctantly trusted. Who had marched from that solar today knowing full well he could not protect her.

He would show her that she *did* need him.

Guy grabbed her head as roughly as he dared and brought his lips crashing down onto hers. Always he'd held something of himself back, but not at this moment. He poured everything into her, kissing her as a starved man would consume the nourishment he needed to survive.

He waited until she gave herself over to him completely, and then, like the savage he was, Guy tore himself away. But he'd not leave her bereft for long.

She wore nothing under the riding gown, and he knew it well. Spinning her around, he divested her of the gown.

When she stood nude before him, he was pleased to realize she did not cover herself this time. Her body was something to be worshiped, its luscious curves begging for him to touch and taste.

"Lie on the bed."

He would have carried her there himself, but Guy did not trust himself to touch her. This would not be a quick coupling, his body's needs be damned. Ignoring the ache that threatened to crush him until he sank deep into her, Guy willed her to do as he asked.

When she did, he groaned aloud, taunted by the clear view of her backside.

Stalking her to the bed, Guy did not waste a moment. He knelt between her legs, opened them and lowered his head.

"What . . ."

He didn't answer. At least not with words. His aim was to show his wife more pleasure than she'd guessed was possible.

Then what?

Nay, not now. This moment was not for contemplation. It was for using his tongue to show Sabine that last eve had been only the beginning.

"People . . . do this?"

He could not laugh at her barely coherent words. But when she reached for his head and lifted her hips to meet him, neither could he continue without completely losing control. Lifting himself above her, he entered her much more swiftly than he had the night before, when her maidenhood had been intact.

Her gasp emboldened him, and her wild eyes nearly made him forget himself.

But he did not. When Sabine cried out his name for the entire inn to hear, he forced himself to pull away, grateful for his foresight in grabbing the cloth near the bed earlier.

Guy barely heard her gasp, but he could discern a distinct and unladylike "My God."

Chuckling at the epithet, he stood and cleaned himself. He planned to lie back down, but Sabine's look stopped him. She might be well-pleasured, but something was amiss.

Afraid to ask, he swallowed back the words—only to ask her anyway a moment later.

"Something is wrong?"

Her nose crunched up in displeasure as Guy sat beside her. The mattress sunk under his weight.

"Aye."

She reached out and laid a hand on his arm.

"Very wrong."

His stomach twisted into knots. Guy had no answer for the question she was about to ask. He needed time to think. To sort through all that had happened. To understand why she hadn't responded to him.

Reaching up and taking a strand of her bright hair in his hand, Guy marveled at the woman sprawled across his bed. "Tell me."

Her lips turned down, and he braced himself for her words.

"I am so incredibly hungry."

Guy laughed at her obvious deception.

"That can be helped, my lady wife."

It was the detachment between his mind and his heart that could not.

CHAPTER 25

"**D**o you feel much improved?"

They sat in as secluded a spot as could be found in the inn's great hall. Braziers stacked with coals from the main hearth kept away the chill that had begun to follow them on their travels. In all, it was a comfortable position, much more so than the previous inn.

"Aye."

They had just finished eating pottage, bread, and cheese. A pitcher of ale had completed their meal.

"You were saying, about de Chabannes?"

Damned if he could remember.

"Guy?"

"You're much too distracting."

Sabine rolled her eyes. "I've done nothing to distract you."

"Mayhap not. But your swollen lips and unkempt hair are doing exactly that." He leaned forward. "I'm reminded of—"

"My hair is not unkempt."

Patrons next to them looked their way. But he cared not. Let them look. He was a lucky man, and Guy could not blame them for their curiosity.

So long as their gazes did not linger, of course.

"Very well," he conceded, nodding his thanks to the serving girl who took away the remnants of their meal. "He's agreed to come here on the morrow. I'd prefer not to bring you either to the camp or Noreham Castle if either can be avoided."

Sabine's top lip glistened as she took a hearty sip of ale. What he wouldn't give to remove the moisture with his tongue.

"And today?"

"His way of reminding me Bande de Valeur is both well-protected and amply compensated. It will take all of Bishop Salerno's funds, and more, to accomplish our goal."

"Can you not simply match whatever amount"— she lowered her voice—"the king has promised?"

Guy wished it were so.

"'Tis not so simple. We both are well aware of how the king deals with those he considers enemies to his rule."

Sabine frowned. "'Tis tricky, to be sure."

He was about to respond when the hairs on his neck rose. Spinning in his seat, Guy turned just in time to catch the unmistakable view of four men wearing the emblem of three lions on their surcoats.

They sat on the other side of the hall, out of Sabine's line of sight.

"What is it?"

His hand moved to the hilt of his sword.

"King's men. Four of them."

Sabine's eyes widened.

"Listen carefully," he said to his wife. "I want you to wait until someone walks by us. When they do, step out in front of them and make your way to the stairs. Bolt yourself inside our room, and do not answer for anyone."

Her eyes widened. "And if they are here for you? For us? Will they not break down the door?"

He watched the table but could see no movement with so many sitting between them.

"If that happens," he said without looking at her, "it means I am dead," he answered honestly. "And will have taken at least some of them with me. I've a knife in the room that I want you to strap to your leg. If you're taken, use it. Escape by any means necessary, Sabine. Imprisonment means death."

He looked toward the men then back to his wife long enough to be sure she heard him.

Though Sabine lost color, she did not flinch. She nodded as if he'd asked if she would like for him to fill her mug with more ale.

"Do you understand?"

She didn't have time to answer.

"Now!"

A serving girl was walking past their table, providing the perfect cover. He watched as Sabine did exactly as he had instructed, using the girl to hide her escape. Guy did not dare to move in any way until she was safely through the door that led to the second floor. Once she was gone, however, he moved quickly.

Using a variation of the trick he'd advised her to use, Guy hid behind a knight and made his way to the edge of the room, where he could see the king's men more clearly. One of the men looked around the hall. Precisely what he'd expect him to do if he were here searching for someone.

Cursing de Chabannes under his breath, Guy prepared to defend himself. Although he had trouble believing the Frenchman would betray him without first hearing the terms he brought, he could think of no other explanation. Perhaps his former company leader had turned him in but not Sabine, although he couldn't rely on that.

He would take the bald man first. He was the largest and most likely to cause real damage. Timely, as he was also the first to stand. His companions followed, and Guy unsheathed his sword as quietly as possible. He'd positioned it along the wall so as not to draw attention to his movements.

Either you kill all four of them or Sabine remains in danger.

Guy was ready.

When the men rushed forward all at once, he turned and nearly raised his sword to greet them. Except Guy belatedly realized they were rushing toward the door of the inn.

Not toward him.

"Lord Berkshire, you are—"

In the ensuing scuffle, Guy could not hear anything but shouts. From the king's men? Lord Berkshire? Before long, both parties had stumbled through the door, the soldiers spiriting their prisoner off into the night.

Following them, Guy attempted to get past the crowd, and he managed to get close enough to see the men had already mounted, the unfortunate nobleman between them. Already whispers reached his ears.

"Not paying his taxes . . ."

"He comes here often. Good man . . ."

"They go too far to arrest such a man as Berkshire."

"His only son killed at Bouvines."

Guy had heard enough. With the king's men well away from him, he made his way through the crowd once more, this time to get back inside.

To assure himself she was safe.

CHAPTER 26

Sabine paced back and forth as Guy and de Chabannes met belowstairs, the room as stifling today as it had been all week. Three days had passed since the incident. After the king's men had come, and de Chabannes had failed to do so, she and Guy had agreed not to venture far. Which meant this room, the hall below, and the inn's grounds had become quite familiar.

Much as she and Guy had become familiar with each other.

Though she still saw glimpses of the arrogant mercenary she'd first met, the Guy who had sat quietly by the fire telling her tales of tourneys and battles was very different. She'd commented on it one night as they supped in the hall.

"Which Guy Lavallis is true?" she had asked, not for the first time, after he grabbed her hand, pulling her up to dance as the fiddler launched into a lively tune.

"This one or the slightly arrogant one who spits at danger and swaggers through every hall as if it is his very own kingdom?"

His answer had been to spin her around.

"Slightly?"

Though they were not the only people dancing, they were easily the most visible. With the caution Guy had been taking lately, it seemed a strange departure.

"I was being kind."

He pulled her close. "Kinder than last eve," he whispered in her ear. Sabine's core clenched in anticipation of his next words. "Do you remember, lady wife? When I asked for a moment's respite?"

"A moment? 'Twas more than a brief moment, and if I recall, your hand had strayed—"

"Ahh, I do remember now. I was surprised to find you wet and ready again so soon."

Sabine looked both ways, mortified by the thought that someone might have heard them. The fiddler had stopped playing, and she tried to sit back down.

Instead, she found herself in Guy's arms, at his mercy.

"I am both men." Sabine shivered at his husky tone. "And did warn you. I am no gentleman."

She disagreed. The only place he was decidedly a mercenary was in bed, where he was merciless in his quest to please her, something he did splendidly well. Yet he still pulled from her each time they lay together. He said nothing about it. But neither did she.

And Sabine knew why.

Guy had spoken more of his desire to form his own company of mercenaries. He admitted he'd turned down offers from two of his friends, Terric and Conrad, to captain their men-at-arms. Although he would have been proud to serve either man, he told her, he didn't like the thought of being rooted to one place.

She understood what it meant. His feelings for her had clearly caught him off guard, but his plans didn't leave room for a wife and a child.

Then again, Sabine had also not expected to meet a man she wished to keep as her husband. She'd become accustomed to the notion she would have to take care of herself.

When the door creaked open now, Sabine nearly ran to Guy. Part of her had feared he would not come back.

But something stopped her. The look on his face, perhaps.

She had never seen him quite so angry.

Slamming the door behind him, Guy proceeded to pace back and forth as she'd been doing.

"He is a bastard," he spat, tossing his sword and scabbard onto the bed on his next pass. "De Chabannes does not intend to make this easy."

"What did he say?"

Sabine sat on the edge of the bed, watching her husband walk to and fro.

"He will consider the offer."

She waited, but Guy said no more.

"And?"

He stopped, ran his hands through his hair, and looked her in the eye. Two large strides brought him to the bed. Sabine thought he intended to kiss her as he leaned down. Instead, he snatched up the recently discarded scabbard, attached it to his belt, and then grabbed his sword.

"He was not at all remorseful for having alerted Lord Noreham to our presence. He said little and agreed only to consider my offer carefully."

He turned toward the door. "I cannot stay here any longer. Come."

Shoving aside her disappointment, she asked Guy where they were going.

"To the village. I dislike the man but don't believe he's told Noreham about our true purpose. We should be safe enough."

Sabine did not remark that her father had said much the same, that she would be safe enough with Lord Burge, when last she saw him. Burge was no longer a threat. And if de Chabannes did not betray them, their only concern was for his decision. If the French mercenary stayed, ready to fight for John, the order's short rebellion would be over.

Or their victory would be much less assured, at any rate. The momentum would turn against them.

We should be safe enough.

She hoped her husband was right.

CHAPTER 27

Guy thanked the smith for sharpening his sword and left the shop. He smiled at the thought of how his friend Lance might react to this blacksmith's disorderly shop. His friend nearly as insistent on keeping order in the smithy as he was of the righteousness of their cause against the king.

"'Tis good to see you smile."

"I thought of Lance," he admitted as he and Sabine moved away from the smithy. The day was hot for September, and the ground unusually dry from a lack of rain.

A good day to explore the village.

"That mark," she said, nodding to his arm. "You said he has one too?"

Guy waited until a group of Noreham's knights moved past. Thankfully, they had not even glanced their way.

"Lance and I met before the others, at an earlier Tournament of the North. My father had commissioned a new sword from his father months earlier."

"His father was also a smith?"

"Aye. One of the best. But a mean bastard too."

Sabine tripped, though Guy could not see any obstacles in front of her. He took her arm anyway, and he found he was reluctant to let go.

So he didn't.

"When I collected my father's sword, I met Lance for the first time."

"And the marking? The fleur-de-lis on your arm?"

He instinctively tightened his grip on her arm, still tucked through his. "A reminder. Lance and I received the marks together. Then later Terric and Conrad followed our lead."

They slowed.

"A reminder of what?"

She looked up at him with such sweetness and sincerity, he could not do aught but answer her.

"The three points commonly represent the three estates. Commoners, nobility, and clergy. 'Tis a reminder we do not accept that. Lance is now lord of Tuleen, but he is also a blacksmith." He shrugged. "I am but a mercenary. Son of a mercenary and a common woman."

"But you will be the leader of men someday."

It was not a question. Sabine said it with such unshakable certainty . . . Her support, her belief in him, made Guy feel as if the sun had come up twice that day.

"Aye," he said simply.

When her eyes widened, Guy turned to see what Sabine was looking at behind him.

His heart sank into his stomach. It was as if their pleasant day had just been catapulted into darkness. He'd seen the look on her face and knew what it might mean.

And Guy simply wasn't ready for it.

۞

SABINE COULD NOT BELIEVE IT.

Despite the size of Noreham Castle, this was not an overly large village. Even in large towns, girdlers would often come for market day and then move on to the next town.

But there it was. A wooden sign bearing the image of a decorative belt chape, swaying back and forth with the breeze.

"Could it be?"

Even as she asked, Sabine knew this was indeed a girdler's shop.

"It would appear so."

She had already pulled her arm from Guy's comfortable grasp. Still incredulous, Sabine ran into the small wooden structure. Belts of all kinds lined every surface. When the older man behind the table looked up from his work, his gaze inquisitive, she remembered her mother's warning.

You've a skill, but that matters little to most men.

Additional words were unnecessary. Sabine knew few women had ever been accepted into a girdler's guild. Her own father, though proud of her handiwork, had never allowed her, or her mother for that matter, to bring her wares to the market. He'd claimed it would be inappropriate due to their station, but Sabine had long suspected that was only a part of what made her father uncomfortable. If they'd been men, he likely would have felt differently.

She watched as the man looked down to her waist as any good girdler would do. Waiting, Sabine sucked in a breath and held it.

After a long moment passed, the white-haired man crooked a finger to her. Sabine took a step toward him, distantly aware of Guy standing just behind her.

"Who made that?"

His voice crackled like dry firewood.

"I made it myself, Master . . . ?"

"Roger."

Roger. Was it his given name or a surname?

"Master Roger."

Sabine looked back at Guy and nearly laughed at his expression. He was glaring at Master Roger as if the man had just proclaimed himself a loyal servant to the king and accused them of being traitors.

And then she realized why.

Locking eyes with him, Sabine only turned back to the girdler when the older man cleared his throat.

"Splendid" was all he said.

Sabine did not know how to proceed. She didn't even know what she wanted from the girdler. Her surprise at seeing him here had overridden all other considerations.

"A girdler's shop in a village this size," she said, realizing she'd not actually asked a question. Or even introduced herself.

But the man's kindly eyes urged her to continue. This was not, she sensed, a man who would reject her simply for being a woman.

"I am Lady Sabine. And this is my husband, Sir Guy Lavallis."

The man's brows drew together. "The mercenary with a sword arm like none other."

She nodded as if she'd had some part in honing her husband's skill.

"Aye," she said, belatedly realizing Guy may not want his name being spread more than necessary. It was likely some might question his presence, especially with Bande de Valeur camped nearby. Though since Noreham already knew, it hardly mattered. But Master Roger said nothing more about Guy.

"My father served the lord of Noreham, and his

father did the same before him. My grandfather built this shop. We have been favored by the lord here, and by God, for many years."

That he could stay in one place without having to travel from market to market was indeed a boon.

"May I?" she asked. When Roger nodded, she began to pick up the pieces arrayed before her. Some leather, some woven braid, and still others made from embroidered fabric and even metal. Sabine picked up a woven silk belt with two decorative metal mountings, one shaped like a rose and the other a woman's head. "'Tis lovely," she murmured.

Sabine hadn't realized so much time had passed, but the next time she looked at Master Roger, he'd finished the belt he had been working on as they entered the shop. Thin leather capped with a belt chape, it looked much like the engraving on the sign.

"I would love to learn this technique," she said, more to herself than the two men in the room.

"How long will you be in the village?" Master Roger asked.

She looked to Guy, but he said not a word.

"I am unsure how long I . . . *we* . . . plan to stay."

"You are welcome to return on the morrow. I had an apprentice who left for London a sennight ago." The girdler shrugged.

Sabine understood. It was well-known that the best girdlers resided in London, but it was also quite difficult to be accepted into the guild that would allow for trade in the city. Her father had promised they would visit one day, but that day had never come.

"I am honored, but 'tis unlikely I shall be able to do so," she said sincerely, knowing Guy would not approve of the plan. It would bring too much attention to her, to them.

"Nay."

She and Roger both turned to Guy in surprise. The single word reverberated throughout the small room.

"If it pleases you to come here, do so."

"You are not opposed to it?"

"I am not."

It seemed to please the girdler that she sought permission from her husband. In truth, she wanted only to ensure the arrangement would be safe.

Smiling at Roger, she agreed to visit the next day. "Many thanks for the offer."

"Until tomorrow, my lady."

On the way out of the shop, Sabine found herself questioning Guy's decision. Being out in public, taking part in the village—it would expose them. Which meant he very much wanted her to apprentice with Master Roger.

Of course he did.

When de Chabannes returned to France, they would part ways. But Sabine knew Guy felt increasingly responsible for her safety. He would feel better about leaving if he knew she had the means to earn coin and practice her art. Then he could gather men for the company he'd dreamed of starting. Travel as he loved to do.

Without the burden of a family.

Neither spoke on the ride back to the inn. Perhaps there was naught left to say.

Unless . . .

Unless she had misread the situation.

"Guy?" she asked, aware of the import of what she was about to say. But Sabine had to know. They'd just dismounted outside of the inn and handed their horses' reins to the stable boy. "Do you wish for me to apprentice with Master Roger so I might remain here? After you leave?"

Sabine's heart thudded so hard in her chest she could hear the sound in her ears. But she wasn't done; she knew she had to be direct. She'd never forgive herself if she didn't at least ask.

Voice quivering, she continued, "Do you still wish to part ways when this is over?"

CHAPTER 28

He'd given her no explanation. Nothing other than a terse "aye," followed by silence.

That night was the first they'd not made love since coming to the inn. Yesterday, the first they'd spent apart. Sabine had gone to Master Roger both days, and she'd found him a kind and patient teacher, and an even more skillful girdler. His tutelage had allowed her to forget, for brief moments, the horrors of the past few months.

Her parents. The abbey. Guy's declaration. His rejection.

She was bathing in the wooden bathtub in their room that second night when a knock came on their door. Guy rushed to answer it, stepping outside to speak with the visitor.

"An invitation to the camp," he announced upon reentering the room.

Guy walked up and handed her the missive.

"This eve."

Sabine read it and handed the parchment back to him, noticing he seemed to have a sudden interest in the bathwater.

Tearing his gaze away, he began to change his clothes. When he pulled up his tunic and a part of the undershirt lifted too, she turned away. Sabine did not need to see more of him. She was already tormented by memories of his body. By the way he continued to look at her even after he'd admitted he still wished for them to separate. Would things have been different had she answered him the other day, when he'd declared himself to her?

She stood in the bath and reached for the drying cloth, only then noticing he was watching her. Shirtless. Muscles poised as if he were prepared to grab her should she run into his arms.

She knew from his expression Guy would not reject her now. Not in this, at least.

He would embrace her. Touch her. Make love to her, to a point.

But then he would pull away from her, a harsh reminder of the temporary nature of their arrangement.

Drying herself, Sabine moved to the bed and began to dress. Refusing to turn to him, she donned her hose and shift. Growing up, she'd always had a maid to help her, but she'd become accustomed to performing her ablutions without any assistance. And so she pulled down the simple kirtle she'd purchased in the village and began to brush her hair.

Which is when she noticed him.

Guy still hadn't moved. And he clearly wanted to say something.

Unable to remain silent any longer, she finally relented. "Do you wish to ask me a question?"

His bare chest filled with air. Finally, he shook his head.

"Do you wish to say something, then?"

She was becoming angry now. How could he look at her like that, his eyes full of heat, after what he'd said?

"Tell me, Guy. Say it," she nearly yelled.

"I . . ."

She dropped her hands from her hair.

"What is it? Please," she pleaded. "Either tell me or do not continue to look at me so."

"I . . ."

For a wild moment she imagined he would say, "I love you." But it was foolish of her to think it. He clearly regretted what he'd said to her the other day. That short answer he'd given her in response to her question about parting—"aye"—was how he truly felt.

He looked at her a moment longer, his gaze tortured, then turned from her.

Sabine wanted to throw the brush at him in frustration. Instead, she gripped it so tightly her hand hurt, though not nearly as much as the poor hair she now abused in anger.

She tried to tell herself to stop, but it was no use.

The simple fact was that she loved her husband. And should have listened to him at the outset. He was no gentleman. Sabine had married a mercenary and now was paying dearly for that decision.

***

"Outrageous."

The amount the mercenary leader had asked for would be impossible for him to deliver, even with the bishop's support, and de Chabannes knew it.

"You must consider the damage to Bande de Valeur's reputation if we were to renege on a promise made to the king."

Sitting next to his wife and across from his former master, Guy tried to remain calm. But he was in the foulest of moods. His silent stand-off with Sabine haunted him. It was his fault, he knew, but that made it no easier. The end result was that he was in no mood for de Chabannes's games.

"I've given you the amount we can pay, and you've

admitted 'tis nearly double what John has pledged. And we both know you don't give a shite about your standing with either king. So tell me, Aceline"—he used his given name apurpose—"what are you about other than to squeeze more coin from me?"

De Chabannes made a noncommittal sound and turned toward Sabine.

"What say you about your husband's treason?"

Guy stood.

But Sabine put her hand on his arm. Reluctantly, he sat back down.

"I am but a servant here," she said, "as you well know."

He didn't like de Chabannes's look. The man knew something, and Guy had a feeling they were about to learn what that something was.

"A servant, you say? Of your husband's? Or your king?"

"Aceline," Guy warned.

"Or perhaps 'tis your late father who possesses your loyalty? Robert de Stuteville was his name, was it not?"

This time, his wife would not waylay him. Guy drew his sword before de Chabannes could even stand.

His former master was quick.

But he was quicker.

"Bastard," he snarled.

De Chabannes tsked. "Is this your preferred manner of negotiation?"

Guy did not put down his weapon.

"Only with those who have betrayed me."

Reaching out a hand, de Chabannes pushed down Guy's sword. He allowed it for one reason—Sabine was watching.

And she was scared. He could see the terror in her eyes, and perhaps it was warranted. Killing this man would do little for their cause other than to ensure the failure of the order's plan.

"I am a servant of England," Sabine said, her voice unwavering.

They both turned to stare.

"'Tis your right to refuse my husband's offer. You may also fault all of us, my father included, for opposing the king's oppression. But Guy spoke of you as an honorable man who would not betray him, so if you will . . . please prove that his words are true."

She lifted her chin in defiance.

"Or not."

This was the woman who had cornered him in the abbey and forced him to marry her.

Perhaps "forced" was too strong a term. He'd never truly been forced to do anything—it wasn't in his nature. Nay, Guy had wanted Sabine as much that day as he did in this moment.

It was a shame he'd made such a mockery of their marriage.

"Very well."

De Chabannes squared his shoulders, and Guy knew in that moment that they had lost. Aceline would not do it. And with Bande de Valeur behind John, the barons who were still undecided would be much less likely to give their support.

"We stay."

He did not give his former master the satisfaction of a response. He'd fought with him for many years and knew no words would sway him.

They'd discovered the one thing more valuable to Aceline de Chabannes than coin.

The king's favor.

A king he did not even call his own. One whose ancestors his people had fought against.

But de Chabannes's own words came back to him.

To be a mercenary is to be loyal to one person. Yourself. Remember it well.

And he did.

Sheathing his sword and taking Sabine's arm, he prepared to walk away. But he did have one question for the man. He had to ask, if only for his wife.

"What will you do with this knowledge?"

He did not have to elaborate.

De Chabannes looked him in the eye. "Ensure there are no repercussions for my choice."

He nodded, their understanding mutual.

None but the order would know Bande de Valeur had been given an opportunity to join the rebellion by leaving England's shores. Sabine would be safe.

Guy would leave Noreham with his head.

But nothing else.

CHAPTER 29

S urely the innkeeper thought it odd that a married couple who'd stayed in the same chamber for many days should suddenly secure a separate chamber. Sabine had made the suggestion three days ago, and for the past few nights, she'd been alone in their original chamber while Guy slumbered in the room next to hers. The only other one in this wing of the inn.

He'd balked at the suggestion at first, but Sabine had reminded him she would soon be completely alone. It would be better, she'd argued, to get used to that fact now.

She'd decided to stay with Roger.

He'd offered her—and Guy—his former apprentice's room above the shop. They'd built it many, many years ago, he and his wife, with the hope it would one day be used by children. But they'd never had any. After his wife's passing, he'd given the room to his apprentice.

When she realized it was loneliness, not obligation, that had prompted him to offer the room, Sabine had decided to accept the offer. But she'd put off sharing her decision with Roger. Once she told him, she wouldn't be able to change her mind without devastating the man, and she still wasn't totally certain about Guy.

Roger had asked her about their background, of course. She'd not wanted to lie to him, so she had offered partial truths. That her family had been killed, her inheritance forfeited. That Guy was a knight without lands of his own.

True enough.

Rather than wait for Guy to escort her, Sabine left her room and walked down to the hall to break her fast. She'd done the same yesterday. He'd reacted with anger, of course, and she'd been quick to remind him that he was the one who wanted them to part. She would have to learn to do things alone. He hadn't accompanied her to the shop after that, nor had she seen him walk past the shop during the day, something he'd done in the past. He had come at sunset to escort her back to the inn, and if Roger had noticed the chill between them, he'd said nothing about it.

"So this is how it will be?"

Sabine spun around at the sound of his voice, hating how the anger reverberated through her body. The thought of never hearing his voice again brought tears to her eyes.

Oh, she wouldn't let herself cry over him. She simply wouldn't. There was no point. She'd asked. He answered. Her husband would soon be leaving, and she refused to beg him to do otherwise.

"I'm not sure what you mean," she said softly, keenly aware of the innkeeper's gaze on them both.

"Until I deem it safe—"

"I should remain in my room. Alone. Staring at the door and waiting for my savior to walk through?"

"Sabine—"

"Did we not have this same discussion yesterday morn? Will we repeat it each day until you leave?"

His eyes flashed, but Sabine was not daunted. Sad, aye. Devastated too. But not daunted.

"You are most anxious for me to do so, it seems?"

She had no answer to that. Of course she did not wish for him to go. She had asked him to stay, had she not?

"I'm no longer hungry."

Turning away from him, Sabine marched through the hall and out into the cool morning mist. She'd brought a cloak today as the weather had begun to turn. It seemed summer was suddenly quite over.

Fitting.

"Sabine?"

Praying for strength, she faced him. Ignored the tic in his jaw. The way his tongue stuck out for the briefest of moments and licked his lips. Ignored, or tried to, the tug on her heart.

"Aye?"

"Stand behind me."

She raised her chin. "Never."

Did he not know her at all? Had he not listened all those times she'd spoken about her role in their relationship? In the rebellion? Stand behind him?

"I beg you, stand behind me."

She would not. Though . . . why would he ask her to do so?

Sabine found herself being hauled to that very spot as if she were a sack of grain. How dare he . . .

Only then did she hear the riders approaching. Peering around her husband, she saw Noreham's men approaching as if their need was urgent. How had no one known they were coming? Still holding her in place, Guy was preparing to draw his sword when one of the men stopped him.

"Desist," he boomed. "We are here only to request your presence at the behest of our lord."

"Our presence?" Guy asked, clearly stalling.

The man who'd spoken looked at her then. "Nay. Yours alone."

She knew what Guy would do before he said a word. Already shaking her head, she continued to do so even as he spoke softly in her ear.

"Go to Roger and stay there. If I am not back by morning, flee."

"No. I am coming—"

"No, you are not. Go."

He intended to sacrifice himself.

Sabine shook her head. "I will not."

"Sabine," he whispered, his lips close enough to her neck for a kiss. "I am sorry. For everything." He slipped something into her hand. "Keep this safe and use it if necessary. Now go."

He did not give her a chance to respond. To ask exactly what he had apologized for. Before she could even say goodbye, her brave husband was walking past the men toward the stable, presumably to get his mount and ride to Noreham.

And likely to his death.

CHAPTER 30

Noreham's men were as silent as the room in which he'd been sleeping at the inn. Alone. Without Sabine.

They passed familiar landscape, skirting the village that had become Sabine's refuge these past days. Even now, as he awaited almost certain imprisonment, he thought of her.

Not the disappointment of having failed his friends.

Not fear for his life.

Not regret for having never sought out his mother so he might tell her what her abandonment had done to him.

Nay, he thought of his wife.

Guy had no doubt she would be resourceful enough to escape. With her own coin and the promissory note from the bishop, Sabine would have plenty of resources to find an appropriate escort to Licheford. And Conrad would keep her safe.

If Noreham had discovered her true identity, surely his men would have taken her as well.

She would be safe.

He repeated it over and over and over again, all the way to the castle and into the keep. Doing so made him forget, at least temporarily, that his short life was likely at an end. Cursing de Chabannes, as he'd done so many times of late, he followed Noreham's men to the stables.

Surprisingly calm given the situation, he did wonder when they would remove his weapon. The men hadn't so much as glanced at his sword, nor had they flanked him.

Odd, that.

Earlier, he'd assumed they knew he would not dare to use it. Sabine had been standing right there with him at the inn. Her presence had ensured his acquiescence. So why did they hesitate now?

Did they know something he did not? Did they have men watching her, ready to retaliate if he should attempt to flee?

"Lavallis."

Noreham joined their small group. The young baron was not armed, and yet his men departed, leaving them alone together.

"Will you walk with me?"

Guy looked for a knife. For any weapon. But Noreham appeared to be completely unarmed.

He followed the baron back outside and through a passageway that led to one of the four stone towers visible from the outer walls. It opened to a long *chemin de ronde,* called a wall-walk here in England. He and the baron stepped onto it, quite alone, and the only guard in sight moved away.

He could kill Noreham with one stroke.

He might even make it away from the keep and through the gatehouse undetected.

But curiosity stayed his hand.

"That would be unwise."

Guy had neither moved nor looked at his sword. He would have smiled then had Noreham not been his enemy.

"Perhaps wiser than bringing me here. Armed. And alone."

"Do you believe so?"

Noreham started to walk, so Guy followed.

That's when he saw them. From this vantage point, the entire Bande de Valeur camp was visible. White tent after white tent. Hundreds of men. The largest mercenary army in the world.

"Why do you believe they are here?" Noreham asked.

Guy did not hesitate.

"To fight for the king. Against his own people."

"John says otherwise."

Guy nearly laughed. "Does anyone believe they are here simply to ensure peace?" He looked Noreham directly in the eyes. "Do you?"

The answer was suddenly as clear as glass. Guy Lavallis might be a famous swordsman, but he was an idiot.

How could he have made such a grave mistake in judgement? Never in his life had he been so unaware, but of course, he knew the answer.

He had misread this situation with Noreham so erroneously because he was deeply in love with his wife. She'd eclipsed everything else.

CHAPTER 31

"**G**o now, my lady."

"But—"

"Ol' Roger never led a battle or defended a castle against a siege. But he's lived three of your lifetimes, and he's tellin' you to go. Now."

Sabine's father had always told her that while it was a mistake to trust the wrong person, it was a much worse error to trust none at all. Though she had coin, along with the promissory note she refused to use under any circumstances since doing so would implicate both Guy and the bishop, Sabine knew no one in town other than Master Roger.

If she hoped to save the man she loved, she needed to get to the Earl of Licheford, and soon. Which meant she required help. Although it chafed her pride to admit she could not go alone, she knew it was so. Time was of the essence.

Teary-eyed and unable to form the words at first, she'd broken down nearly the moment she entered the shop. Sabine had then proceeded to tell Roger everything.

He'd immediately suggested that she hire the services of Eric the Earl.

"My father would never have trusted a man named

Eric the Earl with my safety," she mused. Most especially, she added silently, since he was a disgraced knight and not an earl at all.

"Would he trust me?" Roger pressed.

"Aye. As I do."

"I knew Eric's grandfather. And his father. He'd served the earl until a disagreement put them at odds."

According to Roger, it had been quite the scandal some years ago, though none knew the circumstances behind Eric's dismissal. One day, he'd been removed from the castle. He was never seen speaking to Noreham again. Spending his days in the field with his father and nights training for tournaments, which he still regularly won, Eric began to style himself "Eric the Earl." It seemed a jest between him and, well, himself.

When Sabine reluctantly agreed to his suggestion, Roger left her in the shop to speak with Eric. Sure enough, he was more than willing to escort her.

But Guy had asked her to wait until morning.

She said as much to Roger.

"You admit he is likely in danger," the older man said, insistent. "As are you, my lady. Please do not delay."

She hesitated.

Go to Roger and stay there. If I am not back by morning, flee.

His instructions had been quite clear, and yet . . . if she had not listened to her parents, perhaps Sabine would not have been imprisoned in Holybourne Abbey.

"If Guy comes . . ."

Her words were cut short by Roger, who had circled around his worktable to engulf her in a hug. She squeezed the old man back. Although they'd only spent a few days together, they'd become close none-theless. She would miss him.

"I will tell him."

Eric the Earl had already suggested the best route for them to take to Licheford, which Roger could share with Guy if he did indeed return in the morn.

Oh, please let him return.

Every time she thought of those men on horse-back, staring at her . . . at Guy.

Why had they not taken her if de Chabannes had indeed betrayed them?

Where was Guy at this moment?

It was the answer to that last question that worried her most. For if the worst had happened, he might not even be in Noreham's dungeon. Nay, he might be on his way to London to await the king's displeasure . . .

Sabine shivered.

When she finally made eye contact with Roger, the girdler attempted a smile, though it was the same fixed expression he'd had a couple of days ago, when they'd discussed the room upstairs that had been in-tended for his children, the ones he and his wife had never had. He'd tried to convince her it was just as well he'd never had children. That his happy marriage and the joy his belts gave people had been enough.

But it was a smile filled with regret and edged with a lie that no one believed.

Least of all Sabine.

"GONE?"

Surely he hadn't heard the girdler correctly.

"To Licheford."

Guy froze.

"She told me everything," the man continued.

A chill ran through him, not unlike the one that had finally alerted him to Noreham's true purpose.

He quirked his brow, waiting for Roger to explain. When the man didn't start speaking immediately, he said, "I told her to wait until morn." Impatience gave his voice a hard edge.

"I convinced her it wasn't wise."

Guy's eyes narrowed. "'Tis not a journey I'd have her make without me."

"She's well protected. I ensured it."

Roger had always looked so soft around Sabine, but his face had reverted back to the hard, leery look he'd had that first day they'd wandered into this shop. This was a man who'd faced down trouble many times.

"So you've not been accused of treason, then?" Roger pressed.

Guy did not begrudge his knowledge of their plans, but neither did he wish to speak freely with a man he hardly knew. This was Sabine's confidant. Not his.

"I am here, am I not?"

That earned him another hard look, this one deserved.

"Who did you send with her?"

"A man who was once in Noreham's retinue. She is well protected."

"Once?" Guy's mood was not improving.

"'Tis a long story, one you'd do better to ask the man himself."

If only he could. But Guy was not at liberty to leave just yet. Not before the deed was done.

"She is well protected?" Roger had just said as much, but he needed to be sure.

"She is," the older man answered with certainty.

Guy made for the door.

"Will you go to her?"

Every part of him wanted to say aye. To leave immediately for Licheford. To find his wife, hold her in his arms, and never let go. But he could not do that today, certainly. And maybe not ever. He'd send word to Conrad in the morn, but for now, he had a mission to complete.

With a final farewell, he left the shop and attempted to shrug off the fear that had gripped him the moment he realized she'd left.

I will be alone soon enough. No longer your concern.

How many times had Sabine said those words to him in the past few days? This time, he had no choice but to listen.

CHAPTER 32

"This eve, we will be hosting an important man loyal to our cause." Conrad folded his arms as if he were in his solar rather than on horseback. "He claims to have news."

Sabine slowed her mount to a stop, pulling her mantle tighter across her shoulders. The weather was changing more rapidly this year, the air already cool. Still, the land around Licheford was lovely, and she'd been pleased to accept Conrad's invitation to take a ride.

"Oh?"

On the first morning of her arrival at Licheford, Sabine had not known what to do. Where to go. She was a stranger here, even if she had gotten on well with the earl on her previous visit.

But Guy's friend had been more than welcoming. He'd sent a maid to tend to her needs—a welcome though unnecessary courtesy—broken his fast with her each morn, and included her in every machination dealing with the rebellion.

A sennight had passed without word from Guy.

No news from London either.

If he'd been named a traitor, news of it had not yet reached Licheford, and the small group of men

Conrad had sent out to Noreham to make discreet inquiries had not returned either.

"A man by the name of Stephen Langton," Conrad continued.

Sabine tore her gaze away from the spectacular view around them, rolling green hills that reminded her of home, and looked at the man beside her in surprise.

"The archbishop of Canterbury?" Certainly she'd not expected that.

"Apparently Bishop Salerno spoke to him. He knows of our cause."

Our cause.

Like Guy, Conrad had treated her as a part of the order from the very beginning. It made her want to take a more active role in the rebellion her father had started.

Thinking about the rebellion, and more what could be done, was preferable to thinking of Guy. To wondering if he still lived.

Waiting here, not knowing what had become of him, was as excruciating as it had been waiting for her parents at Lord Burge's residence.

"Think of the importance of this meeting instead," Conrad said.

She didn't need to ask for clarification. He had been watching her, and must have noticed her far-off look.

"I wasn't thinking of Guy, but of my parents."

Conrad's sigh spoke of both sadness and understanding. She wanted to ask more about the circumstances surrounding his own parents' deaths, but it would feel wrong to pry. Instead, she asked another question that had been on her mind for some time.

"The day you met." She looked out at the heathland's purple and yellow flowers, knowing they would soon be gone for the season. "The day you all met, Terric's sister . . ."

Sabine stopped. She was unsure how to ask the question. Even though she and Conrad had shared confidences, it was still a very personal question. And certainly they had more important matters to attend to with the archbishop of Canterbury on the way.

But she could not banish the image of a young girl quailing from an older man's violent attack. Her father had warned her about the possibility of being taken advantage of . . . but she'd never truly considered it until the safety of her home had been taken from her. Then, it had seemed an ever-present concern. And while she trusted Roger, those first few nights traveling here with Eric . . .

She shuddered at the direction of her thoughts.

Conrad was watching her.

"Cait."

They'd become friends, brothers, defending this woman's honor, but Guy rarely spoke of her.

"'Tis the first I've heard her name."

Sabine had not meant to stare at Conrad's scar. He touched it with the tips of his fingers. It happened so quickly, she wondered if he even realized he'd done it.

Sabine forced herself to look elsewhere.

"I've not seen her since that day."

"Did she ever marry?"

Conrad shook his head. "Nay."

They fell into an easy silence then, Sabine thinking of her own marriage. Though Conrad had insisted she remain at Licheford for the interim, she refused to stay indefinitely. But as Conrad had said, the future was as uncertain for every single member of the order. He'd convinced her to think only of the present, an easy task with Guy's whereabouts still unknown.

"We should return to the keep."

"Of course."

He would want to prepare for what promised to be an interesting meeting. Stephen Langton had been exiled to France years earlier by King John, who'd refused to recognize his appointment. Langton had been allowed to return to England after a bitter negotiation, and John's relationship with the pope had suffered because of it.

Some said the archbishop, despite his public declaration in support of the king, privately held a grudge against him. If he was coming here after speaking to Salerno, it would appear those rumors were true.

Which meant more people were learning of the rebellion. They needed the support, of course, but the more people who learned about the order, the more dangerous their position became. Each of them, Sabine included, would become a target. Of course, she'd been one already, and her husband with her.

Urging her mount to a gallop, Sabine caught up with Conrad just as she saw the riders approaching.

⚜

"I'VE NEVER SEEN SUCH TAPESTRIES BEFORE."

Sabine still had difficulty believing she sat one seat away from Stephen Langton, the famed archbishop of Canterbury. Some called him one of the first rebels to King John's rule. Others argued his beliefs were too radical, even among those who despised the current king's practices.

"'Tis good to be back."

"His Grace has been in Burgundy these past years, am I correct?" Conrad said, a rather polite way of asking about his brief banishment.

The meal long since over, they still sat at the high

table. Sweetmeats had been brought and placed before them, but none indulged. The hall had remained bustling for a time, due to the earl's continued presence, but Conrad had dismissed his retainer. And then he'd dismissed the servants too.

Sabine had thought the men would retire to a more private chamber, perhaps the solar, but neither seemed inclined to do so. Which was just as well for her as Sabine very much wanted to be a part of this discussion.

Powerful, at times hot-tempered if Guy were to be believed, but always in control, the earl was unlike any man she'd ever met. A lifetime ago, she'd have seen him through the eyes of an unmarried maiden. At least, her father certainly would have. But there was only one man for her.

There was only Guy.

Her heart lurched as it did each time she thought of him. Wondering where he was. If he was safe. In pain. *Alive.*

"Sabine?"

"I apologize, Your Grace." Thankfully, she'd heard the conversation through her thoughts. "I've heard little of Pontigny Abbey"—she allowed herself a private smile—"though I do have more experience with abbeys of late."

He raised his brows.

"I was pledged to St. Andrew Holybourne Abbey before escaping, much to my overlord's dismay, with Guy Lavallis. The mercenary." She would not apologize for it.

"Your father would be quite proud, I do believe."

She leaned forward in shock, ignoring Conrad between them.

"You knew my father? But you've not been in England these many years."

"Have I not?"

The plump man, his face saggy in the cheeks, smiled. And Sabine immediately understood. He had been in England, though not officially. And he knew her father because both men opposed the king. Their network had been stronger, more extensive, than Sabine had realized.

"That you should be here, at Licheford, is fitting, my dear."

She blinked as he turned his attention to Conrad.

"Your order"—she saw Conrad stiffen at the direct reference to his secret—"is gaining support." He gave them each a knowing look. "And notice."

"If Salerno had not told you—" Conrad started.

"I suspect another would have," Langton finished. "But now, at least, we have a defined course."

"We?"

The Earl of Licheford said that one word with all of the arrogance of a man in his position. Rare, from what she'd observed, for Conrad. But he was indeed an earl, albeit a young one.

"Aye. We."

Sabine had met many noblemen throughout her life, but even their power paled in comparison to the archbishop's. She was not fooled by his affability.

Stephen Langton was not a man to trifle with.

"I've uncovered a document." He lowered his voice despite the lack of company in the ornate hall. "One granted by King Henry, which, though never enforced, could be useful to us now."

Sabine listened as Langton outlined the provisions in a document he called the Charter of Liberties. If John agreed to sign it, to agree to its terms, it would negate some of the powers he now abused. A widow could not be denied her dowry. Children would not be required to purchase land and titles due to them by inheritance. So many of its terms seemed simple but would have far-reaching effects on the governance of their country.

"He will never do it," she blurted.

Both men stared.

"His alternative is to forfeit the crown," Conrad said.

His words brought the situation home for her in a way that nothing else had. Would they truly go to war with their own king?

Aye, if that was what it took. They'd come too far to turn back now, and she had to believe John could be defeated, even with Bande de Valeur at his back. But it would take more coin, more men and . . . dear Lord. They spoke of overthrowing their king by force.

"Do you believe he would agree?" she asked the archbishop.

"I do not know," he said, the honesty in his words highlighted by a deep frown. "I do not know," he repeated, picking up a silver goblet of fine French wine. "But, for the sake of our country, I dearly hope he does."

All three of them fell silent then. A wave of longing washed over Sabine, more intense for their discussion. Guy should be here. To discuss this matter. To hold her. To make love to her. To be her husband.

The part of Sabine that had feared needing him, or anyone, had retreated. Was it so horrible to be loved and protected by a man? When that man was Guy Lavallis? The answer was clearer now than it had been before coming to Licheford.

Unfortunately, she feared it might be too late.

CHAPTER 33

When Licheford Castle rose before him, Guy stopped. Something he'd done little of since leaving Noreham. He'd ridden hard, likely too hard, to get here. Consoling himself that his message must have arrived ahead of him, Guy took a deep, calming breath, Arion dancing under him.

Almost there.

He'd been haunted by the memory of the last time he'd seen Sabine. The look of terror on her face. The horror he'd felt at the notion that she might be hurt on his account.

He'd known then but still had not admitted it. Everything had become clear to him in his conversation with Noreham.

Guy was not so foolish to think he could live without Sabine, the woman he had very deliberately pushed away. He could only hope it was not too late.

Spurring his horse forward, this brief hesitation his last, Guy finally thundered through the gatehouse after startling the poor guards with his shouts demanding entry. He sped past scared servants and more than one of Conrad's retainers, who looked at him as if the devil had just ridden through the gates.

Which was not terribly far from the truth.

Since that day at the tournament, he'd been to Licheford many times. They knew him here, as they did Terric and Lance, but that did not mean his mad run through the courtyard would go unnoticed. It was only when he burst into the hall to find it empty that he stopped to consider she might not be here.

Roger had confirmed this as her destination. But had she made it to Licheford safely? Had she already left?

"Guy?"

He spun around at the voice.

Conrad crossed his arms, looking decidedly angry. "You are alive."

He searched frantically for Sabine.

"Where is she?"

"Tell me how you come to stand here, unharmed. Did you pass the archbishop as you left? And where are the men I sent to Noreham?"

"Archbishop? Men?"

"Aye. When Sabine arrived—"

His knees buckled under him. "She's here?"

"When she arrived with word of your capture, I sent a contingent of men to assess the situation."

"Where. Is. She?"

And then, finally noticing Conrad's expression, he added, "I know not about your men. They never arrived at Noreham, or if they did, I was not aware of it."

"Guy?"

He'd begun to convince himself he would never hear her voice again. Spinning toward the heavenly sound, he took in her deep purple gown and the hair piled artfully atop her head. Sabine looked every bit the noblewoman he did not deserve.

He did not hesitate.

Guy ran to her, reaching his wife in four strides.

He engulfed her in an embrace so tight he couldn't be sure if the sound she made was from joy or pain.

"I was so worried."

She pulled away, her cheeks streaked with tears.

"*You* were worried? What happened? What took you so long?"

Clearing his throat but unwilling to let her go, Guy forced back tears.

Conrad had not moved. Nor had Guy's reunion with his wife softened his expression.

"We thought you dead. Or worse."

Guy chuckled at the utter ridiculousness of his friend's statement.

He noticed, for the first time, they were not exactly alone. In fact, the hall was brimming with people who did not hide their interest in the scene before them.

"My solar," Conrad demanded.

Still, Guy couldn't bring himself to let her go. He wrapped his fingers through hers and squeezed.

She was safe.

Following Conrad into his private chambers, he chose a bench rather than his typical chair. And pulled his wife nearly onto his lap.

"I'm not sure why I continue to be surprised by your antics," Conrad said, brows raised.

Guy ignored him.

Reaching up to grasp a lock of Sabine's hair, he twirled it through his fingers. She had to forgive him for acting like a stubborn arse before they were separated. He'd talk to Conrad later about the idea he'd had on the way to Licheford. But first . . . he had something to tell them.

"Bande de Valeur have returned to France."

CHAPTER 34

S abine was sure her expression of shock matched Conrad's.

It was difficult to think with Guy sitting next to her, touching her. Even if it was just her hair. The gesture brought her as much comfort as she knew it brought him. And though she was still contemplating killing him for making her worry, she sensed something had changed between them.

But for now, she needed an explanation. They'd both been so sure de Chabannes wouldn't bend. What could have changed?

Eyes sparkling, Guy said, "Noreham is with us."

She thought of the young lord whose father had served the king. "Impossible."

He'd come off as so devout. So loyal.

When Guy's eyes met hers, all thoughts of Noreham flew from her head for a moment. So much promise in his eyes . . .

"Ahem."

She spun her head, looking guiltily at Conrad.

"I thought the same," Guy said, responding to her remark. "Thankfully, I did not attempt to kill the man before he explained."

"Kill him? Did he not disarm you at the inn?"

Sabine thought back, attempting to remember exactly what had transpired.

"He did not. By the time I was within his walls, alone, part of me knew something was amiss." He shrugged. "The other part of me thought to kill him before being tossed in Noreham's dungeon."

Having seen Guy's sword arm in action, Sabine had no doubt he could have easily done so.

"He claims there are others like him, openly loyal to John but privately irate with his policies. The election of des Roches as his justiciar was the point at which Noreham turned."

Sabine shook her head. "My father said many of the barons despised the bishop of Winchester nearly as much as they did John's taxes."

"Precisely," Guy continued. "When John asked"— Guy inclined his head—"demanded the use of Noreham's land for Bande de Valeur, he had no choice but to acquiesce. He claims, if necessary, he'd have turned his own men against the company rather than allow de Chabannes's men to fight us."

"You believe him?" Conrad asked.

"I do."

The room was silent.

"He'd begun to suspect our true purpose."

Sabine could guess how events had unfolded after she left. "You and Noreham both convinced de Chabannes?"

Guy winked at her, and the expression of complicity made her heart sing. This was their fight.

Together.

"Aye, lady wife. We did." He looked at Conrad. "Between the bribe I'd already offered him and the knowledge that his host was prepared for a fight . . ." Guy frowned. "He's many things, but Aceline is not a stupid man."

Sabine allowed the news to penetrate.

Noreham was one of them.

He'd threatened Bande de Valeur with a battle, and Guy had offered them twice as much coin as the king. These were not the actions of men who dipped their toes in a rebellion. Like her father, they were prepared to die for this cause. Noreham, for reasons she did not yet know. Guy, as a part of his bond of friendship with the order. And she . . .

Sabine had as much reason to despise John and his rule as any, but she'd never imagined being a part of the movement that would depose him. Or, at the very least, force him to reform.

It was more than she ever could have hoped for that day at the abbey, when the mercenary's conversation had reached her ears.

Much, much more.

Guy watched her.

"Did you see them leave?" she thought to ask.

"Aye. 'Tis what took me so long. Which is why I sent word ahead."

Her brows furrowed. "Nay," she argued, "you did not."

Conrad cut in then. "Who did you send?"

They looked at each other then, all likely thinking the same thing. Guy never answered. He didn't need to. The message never reached them. And in the game of kings, there were rarely any winners. The moves they'd made these past weeks, while necessary, were no longer secret.

"It doesn't matter." Conrad sat back, crossing his arms. "The king will likely notice the absence of his sellswords."

"But he doesn't know the identity of the men who are behind the unification of his opposition," she said as Guy rubbed the palm of her hand with his thumb.

"Yet," Conrad said.

"And women," Guy added.

At another time that would have made her smile, but she knew it wouldn't be long before they were unmasked. Too many people knew for the secret to remain in the dark much longer. Guy. Conrad. Lance. Terric.

Her father would have been proud to know them.

"I would speak to Conrad for a moment." Although she didn't wish to leave, she was swayed by the plaintive tone in Guy's voice. He released her hand, and she stood and left.

"Do not venture far," he said as she walked through the door. "We need to talk."

๑๕๛

"Where are we going?"

Since emerging from Conrad's solar, Guy had been acting . . . odd. She'd assumed he would want to speak to her at once, but instead he'd disappeared, leaving her with the earl. Who had promptly led her out of the solar, their destination unknown.

"I'm sworn to secrecy."

Sabine rolled her eyes.

"And I suppose you'd never break an oath with a member of the order."

Conrad smiled at her as they made their way across the small courtyard, making her scowl in return. The man had refused to tell her anything.

Where Guy had disappeared to.

Where they were going now.

Why Guy had asked for her to leave.

She wondered if his other friends were equally infuriating.

"But supper . . . ," she started, reminding him that the rest of Licheford was even now preparing for the meal. One they could not begin without the earl.

"Can wait."

Sabine stopped trying. She did not fully understand Guy's bond with the other men of the order. Although she'd always wished for a sibling, it had never happened, and her friendships had never been as close as the brotherhood shared by these four men.

To her surprise, Conrad led her into a building she immediately recognized as the smithy. Guy stood there next to a bulky man who was presumably Licheford's master smith. Wielding the smith's iron hammer had given him much the same physique as the two much younger men.

"A woman?"

Both Conrad and Guy gave the man a look that had him staring down at his feet.

"Master Irwin, will you pardon us a moment before we begin?" Guy asked. Although it was not really a question. When the older man walked out, Conrad left them too.

"'Tis not where I'd imagined our reunion," Sabine said.

He reached her so quickly, she had no time to react. His kiss was unlike any of the others they'd shared. It was both strong and soft. Passionate and loving. It answered the question she'd had since Guy returned. And well before that, really.

Sabine kissed him back, only to find herself bereft of his company once more.

"I love you, Sabine."

She hadn't known what to expect, walking in here with Conrad, but it had never occurred to her that he might profess his love.

But she would accept it nonetheless.

"I am so sorry for the answer I gave that day. I should have told you the truth. That I do not want to part with you ever again. That I would be proud to call you my lady wife for the rest of my days. But"—he swallowed—"I've little to offer you. The life of a merce-nary . . ." He shook his head. "Conrad has agreed for us to remain here. If we are still alive when this is done."

He looked at her with such expectation, but Sabine knew what her answer had to be.

"No."

His stricken expression prompted her to clarify her answer.

"You—we—cannot stay here. You're not meant for that life, and I would see the world with you instead."

"My mother—"

"I am not your mother," she said as gently as pos-sible. "And you know it well."

He was still afraid. She could see it in his eyes.

"I would not leave you or our child, if God grants one into our care." Sabine cupped his face in her hands. "Do you hear me, Guy? Never. That is my vow to you. I will never leave."

She poured everything she was into those words.

"I love you enough to accept that I need you," she continued. "More than that, I want you. By my side." Did she dare be so bold? "In my bed."

"Sabine . . ."

"I know."

And she did. Sabine had enjoyed the time she'd spent with Master Roger—it had given her a glimpse of the life that could be—but she'd found something she wanted more.

When Guy pulled off his linen shirt, Sabine could not have been more surprised.

"I don't believe this is a good time"—her eyes fell to his stomach—"or place for . . ."

Her boldness, apparently, had its limits.

"And Conrad is just outside."

Guy grabbed her hand and placed it on his arm.

Just over the marking that bound him to Lance. Covering her hand with his, Guy held her gaze.

"This mark was once a symbol, a reminder that there are those who do not fit so nicely into the three pillars of society. Lance and I . . . are different. But so are Conrad and Terric. They are lords. Wealthy men of great influence who chose to befriend a blacksmith and a mercenary. Men who now risk themselves for a cause bigger than any of us individually."

"What are you saying?"

"This"—he squeezed her hand—"means more now that each of us has marked ourselves with the symbol."

"You mean to say everyone in the order has one?"

Guy nodded, then released her hand.

"The smith made Conrad and Terric's, though theirs are hidden to the world. And he would make yours too."

The smith.

The man standing outside even now.

Did that mean . . . did Guy bring her here to . . .

"Do you mean for me to be marked as you are?" She shook her head. "I was not there that day," she pointed out. "I'm not one of you."

Guy smiled. "But you are."

Her gaze moved back to the table where a wooden block and a metal dish filled with black powder sat. Guy meant for her to bear their mark. To be . . .

"The Order of the Broken Blade," he said. "You were not there then, but you are here now, when it matters. This is as much your father's fight as it is ours, Sabine. I'd ask to marry you, but we're already married. This . . ."

His voice trailed off, but no words were needed. She understood clearly the significance of what he was asking.

Guy cared for those men more than anyone. He loved them.

She looked into his eyes.

He loved her too. Enough so that he'd invited her to join the circle that was more precious to him than life.

Sabine's eyes flew to his arm.

"You can choose to put it anywhere."

So that was what had shocked the smith. Indeed, Sabine had never seen such a marking on a woman. Though it seemed . . . fitting.

"Anywhere?"

When Guy dropped his gaze to her bosom, his smile fled. "Perhaps not anywhere. I would prefer neither Conrad nor his smith see more of my wife than I shall see this night."

He emboldened her.

"Do not concern yourself overly, husband. I plan for you to see quite a bit before the evening is through."

CHAPTER 35

Guy could not have been more pleased.

Nay, that was not exactly true. He'd be more pleased if this blasted meal would end so that he might finally take Sabine to bed. She and Conrad could continue their talk later.

"If you continue to look at your wife as if you would devour her, you're more apt to scare than seduce her," Conrad quipped.

Sabine's laugh almost made him forget they were in the midst of a very dangerous game.

"What do you know of seducing women?"

They sat on a raised dais at the back of Licheford's great hall, the angle encouraging far too many of Conrad's men to glance up at Sabine. He couldn't very well challenge each one of them and supposed he must become accustomed to such glances. She was a beautiful woman.

But she was also his.

Irrevocably, undeniably his.

"I know less than you, my friend."

Conrad was in a more jovial mood than expected, given the circumstances.

"You seem—" Guy struggled to find the right word.

"Relaxed," Sabine provided.

Apparently she'd gotten to know Conrad some. "Aye. Unusually so."

The earl was normally much more . . . rigid. He was also their leader, and Guy would follow him into battle without question. And likely would before this was done.

"I was thinking of how John will react to news of de Chabannes's defection."

They all grinned at that.

"He will be furious," Guy said.

"Incensed," Sabine agreed. "What do you think he will do?"

He'd hoped to wait at least a day to have this discussion. When Guy reached for a piece of meat on their shared trencher, their fingers touched.

Tonight.

He promised with a look, and she smiled back at him.

"He will blame Noreham. Which is why he'll not find him easily."

Neither Conrad nor Sabine asked where Noreham was headed, nor would Guy have answered in such a setting. They were far enough away from the closest table not to be overheard, but still. Uttering such a thing aloud in mixed company would serve no purpose.

Noreham was safe, for now.

But he'd also be branded a traitor. A moniker his new friend was willing to accept, for a time.

"We're not safe anywhere," Guy said, speaking a truth they all knew. None of them had forgotten the missing courier. "He will make the connection, if he has not already. Me. Both of you. All of us. The order is no longer a secret."

Conrad sighed. "We never expected it to remain so."

All three of them remained silent for a time. They ate, Guy unable to resist glaring at a young knight who seemed much too curious about his wife.

"We've enough men to fight, Guy."

He didn't realize the earl had been watching him.

Giving his attention to his ale, Guy finished the meal. As the tables were cleared, he asked after Sabine's shoulder.

"'Tis painful, aye," she admitted. "But much less so than waiting for your return."

"I am sorry for it," he said sincerely. "None of this will be easy."

The mood had shifted, the reality of what they'd done—and were prepared to do—settling over them like an unwanted blanket on a hot day. But they could not kick it off. Not yet. Maybe not ever.

"A toast." Conrad stood, his voice booming. "A toast," he called even louder, quieting the crowd. "To my friend, Sir Guy Lavallis, and his wife, the beautiful Lady Sabine. And to Licheford. May we enjoy this night for what it offers. Life."

Some appeared slightly confused by the toast. They likely had no notion of what was coming. But they would soon enough.

Others, Conrad's captains and the men privy to his private dealings, lifted their mugs with more gusto. If called upon to do so, they would fight for Conrad. Or prepare for a siege against their own king.

They knew not what tomorrow would bring. Nor did Guy.

But he would take his friend's advice. They would concern themselves tomorrow with tomorrow. For tonight was his.

He looked at Sabine.

Tonight was *theirs*.

And he'd not waste a moment of it.

CHAPTER 36

She'd lain awake in this chamber night after night, thinking of him. Worrying for him. Wondering if he were alive or dead.

Now, she was filled with eagerness—and impatience—as she waited for him to join her. When he'd attempted to retire with her, she'd encouraged him to stay belowstairs for a few moments longer so that she might prepare for him.

The maid Conrad had sent to her on that first day had retired after helping her disrobe. The fire had already been stoked, the candles lit. Sabine had nothing to do now but wait.

Wait and think.

She'd known for some time she did not wish to part with her husband, but she'd been prepared to do just that. Although it was highly unusual for a woman of noble birth to make her way alone, she felt confident she could have managed it.

Which didn't mean she truly wanted to.

There would be challenges ahead, but they would face them together. Presently, though, her greatest challenge was calming her racing heart.

Guy nearly split the door in two opening it.

She had no time to react.

He slammed the heavy wooden door shut and descended on her. Grabbing the back of her head, his fingers wrapped through her hair, using it to pull her closer. His tongue demanded entry, and she gladly gave it.

Despite the roughness of his embrace, his lips were gentle, and she gripped him with both hands, bringing him closer.

They melded into each other. Though Sabine could feel her thin shift being pulled from her body, she definitely did not remember Guy removing his shirt.

Or had she done that?

A very short time later, both she and her husband were divested of their clothing.

She didn't expect him to step back. Away from her.

"Look at you."

And he did.

Slowly.

Her core clenched in anticipation as she watched his expression. When he stepped forward this time, he touched her with such gentleness, it raised the hair on her arms.

At least, she imagined it to be so.

He guided her toward the bed as gently as a falconer with a new peregrine. He laid her down on the bed and covered her completely.

But then he stopped.

Poised over her, his arms straining with the effort, he leaned down and kissed her again.

No words were needed, as Guy's tongue told her what to do. To meet his touch. To give herself over to him completely.

And she did.

But Sabine wanted more.

She reached down, covering his buttocks with her hands. Squeezing them, she pressed him toward her.

But her husband refused to be rushed. He continued to make love to her mouth until every inch of her screamed in protest. Her nipples grazed his chest they were so hard. She lifted one leg, bending it at the knee, and attempted to force him into her that way.

Finally, when she couldn't stand it any longer, Sabine reached between them and grasped the length of him. The guttural sound from his throat told her all she needed to know.

He wanted this as much as she did.

As he'd done in the past, Sabine guided him into her. His groan of pleasure eventually broke their kiss.

"God, Sabine."

He helped her, finally, until they were, at last, joined.

But her stubborn husband still refused to be rushed.

He brought his lips down to hers once again, but this time their tongues followed the rhythm of their joined bodies. Slow. Too slow.

She ran her hands down his sides, Guy's shiver her only indication that he noticed. When she grasped his buttocks this time, it was not with gentle guidance but with a firm purpose.

Simultaneously pulling him toward her and thrusting her hips upward elicited the reaction she'd been attempting to provoke all along.

"You're not so subtle tonight," he said, pumping into her with the kind of force she'd been begging for. Coupled with the circular movements of his hips, Sabine was finally content.

Or would have been had her shoulder not suddenly screamed in pain as it rubbed against the mattress.

"What . . . oh."

Realizing the mark of her membership in the order was to blame, Guy did not hesitate. He flipped them around so easily she momentarily wondered if he'd made that move before.

"Better?"

She nodded.

"It won't be sore for long."

Sabine didn't care, as long as they were still joined. And they were. A fact she remembered when Guy thrust his hips forward. She rather liked this particular position. She could see his face. His chest. His shoulders.

All of him.

And enjoyed every bit of it.

Sabine found a rhythm of her own and set a new pace. Shoulder forgotten, she tossed her head back as Guy's fingers found the top of her sex, just above where they were joined. That pressure, along with the rest of it, pushed her to the verge.

"Guy . . ."

"Go ahead, love."

Tremors took her body, and she let them.

Just as she remembered . . .

"Oh no, never again."

Instead of pulling from her, Guy pressed inside even harder. When he found his release a moment later, it was an entirely new feeling. She watched in fascination as his eyes opened, no longer clenched shut as they'd been a moment ago.

Sabine collapsed against him then and decided they would stay in this bed forever. All day. All night. They would never leave.

"I love you, Sabine."

She managed to lift her head.

"And I love you. I'm glad you took me with you that day."

"I'm glad you asked, my bold lady wife."
"Bold? I shall show you what the word means."
Sabine intended to fulfill her promise that night.

CHAPTER 37

G uy groaned at the sound.

Only one person would knock that loud, and he would kill him.

Despite the banging, Sabine was still asleep. Swinging his legs over the side of the bed, Guy reluctantly got up and tossed on a shirt and braies before answering his friend's early morning call.

Indeed, it was Conrad on the other side of the door.

"Come with me," Conrad said, the words simple but his expression less so.

Guy glanced back at his wife, who had just peeked her eyes open.

"I will return shortly," he said, reluctant to leave. The previous night had been, unequivocally, the best of his life.

Her smile the only answer he needed, Guy shut the door behind him.

"A report from the north," Conrad said in an undertone.

Some would say Licheford was in the north, but not those who resided along the border. Concerned, he followed his friend into a chamber he'd never seen before. It was the lord's chamber, he quickly realized, one Conrad himself should occupy. But he did not.

He'd never asked why before, but as soon as Guy stepped into the room, he knew the answer. It was pristine, as if his parents had stepped away moments ago. They'd been dead for five years.

A chill ran up his spine. But when Conrad sat on one of the wooden chairs before the hearth, seemingly quite comfortable, Guy followed suit.

It was a handsome chamber, the large bed worth more than some small manors, no doubt. Even the chairs on which they sat were so intricately carved that Guy was reluctant to touch the engravings.

"So early?"

"Apparently the messenger was told not to rest until this found my hands." Conrad handed him the missive. "And he is not our only early morning visitor. The men I sent after you finally returned."

He read it, silently thanking his mother for at least this one thing. Most men he knew could not read, but she'd insisted he learn to read in both French and English despite the cost of a tutor.

"How is he the first to learn of this?"

It astounded him how Terric, a Scot, continued to be a primary source of information on their English king.

"He's well-connected" was all Conrad said. Which was true. Terric's English earldom afforded him credibility and influence in England. Like his father, Terric found the earldom difficult to maintain while attending to his clan. Wherever he resided, the other complained. With the current troubles, Terric had not been back to Bradon Moor since the previous spring.

"As is John, apparently."

The missive was not good news.

Conrad took back the letter. "Langton alluded to this possibility."

"But you said he did not believe the pope would support John."

Conrad shrugged. "Apparently he was wrong."

"A setback, to be sure."

Terric's message was short but very clear.

By pledging himself to a Crusade, the king had garnered support from Pope Innocent III, an action that would make it nearly impossible for them to gain future support from the barons.

"Will some of those who have pledged to us withdraw their support?"

Guy wasn't sure why he asked the question as he already knew the answer.

"Undoubtedly."

Conrad crumpled the parchment and tossed it across the room as he stood.

Muttering a string of obscenities, he paced back and forth until Guy could stand it no longer. "Will you sit?"

Conrad glared at him. "You manage to send Bande de Valeur back to France, a feat that none actually thought possible—"

"I appreciate your confidence in my efforts."

"You know as well as I do it was always going to be difficult, if not impossible."

Guy smiled despite Conrad's pacing. "Then it appears you sent the right man. Though I wonder, if you had not sent me to St. Andrew . . ."

"You mean"—Conrad sat back down—"if I'd gone instead or sent Terric."

"Bloody hell, brother."

Finally, a smile from Conrad.

"I hadn't thought about that at all." Guy shuddered. "Until now."

"I do believe she would be Sister Sabine by now."

Guy grunted. "Because neither of you would have been so bold as to accept the lady's offer?"

"Nay, because neither Terric nor I would have been foolish enough to allow ourselves to be overheard with such an important message."

"Remind me why I'm here in this chamber with you rather than in a bed with my wife?"

"We need a plan."

"Which actually means you have a plan and will kindly share it with me so I can return to Sabine."

Guy knew he was playing with the earl's patience.

One of his favorite things to do. Every year, the men of the order had reunited at the Tournament of the North. And Guy had quickly learned he was uniquely qualified to goad their fearless leader.

For his own enjoyment, and for that of the other men.

All but Conrad, of course.

"I do have an idea."

"Of course you do."

Conrad ignored him. "Using the archbishop's document, we gather our supporters to alter the old Charter of Liberties and swear an oath to acknowledge the rights we're demanding."

"And demand a meeting with the king?" Guy finished.

"Aye, and demand that he sign and support the new charter."

"If he refuses to meet us?"

"Then we fight."

"And if he meets but refuses to sign the document?"

"We fight."

Guy leaned forward. "The most likely scenario is that we will be fighting against our king before long."

Conrad looked him square in the eyes. "Aye. It would seem so."

"We'll be lucky to maintain our numbers in the face of the pope's support for John."

"Aye."

"If it does come to battle?"

They'd discussed the possibility, of course, but now that the outcome seemed more certain . . .

"We will appeal to Prince Louis."

For most Englishmen, the idea of involving the French monarch in their country's affairs would be as appealing as facing a life of imprisonment in the Tower. But Guy was not any man. His loyalties were to those he loved. And to that end, he would appeal to anyone, including his mother's king.

"Then let it be done."

Conrad looked as if he were chewing small rocks. His friend was torn, and Guy could clearly see it. He leaned forward far enough to clasp Conrad's shoulder. "It is more easily accepted if you consider the end goal rather than the means by which we achieve it. John must be stopped. You know it well, my lord."

He used the title intentionally. For this man, Guy would kneel if asked, and Guy wanted to remind him of the fact.

"I will tell Sabine. When do we leave?"

Before he could remove his hand, Conrad clasped it in his own.

"You are a good man. Sabine is as lucky as you are, brother."

When Conrad released him and stood, Guy didn't move. Nor did he get up when the earl opened the chamber door and left. He sat there, thinking of the discussion he was about to have with his wife, with whom he'd only just reunited.

The days ahead would be dangerous. They could be caught at any time. She risked her life as surely as the four of them did, every day from this day forward.

And yet . . .

He smiled, standing.

They would do it together.

"An abbey," Guy whispered. "Seems fitting we should find ourselves here, does it not?"

"We're being watched," Sabine whispered back, her attempts at keeping Guy quiet not very successful.

They stood with some of the most powerful men in England in this small abbey, waiting for Conrad to speak. As was his custom, her husband refused to submit to the seriousness of the situation. Instead, he leaned toward her as if to whisper something but instead kissed her just behind the ear.

None saw it happen as they were positioned near the back left of the chapel. Conrad stood near the altar, Terric sat behind them and to the right, and Lance had chosen a seat directly in the middle—each of their order placed strategically so nearly every man in the room could be reached quickly. She'd asked Conrad if he really believed one of their own would turn against them. After all, these men had risked their land and titles, their lives, to be here on this cold November day.

"If one or more is actually loyal to John and not the cause, I would be prepared for it," he had said.

According to Guy, it was a part of Conrad's nature

to be suspicious, but she supposed such caution was necessary when plotting treason against the king.

"We are not being watched," Guy whispered back. "Everyone watches Langton. I don't believe they thought he would really attend."

But the archbishop of Canterbury was indeed present.

As were more than twenty barons and six earls, including Conrad and Terric. She spotted Noreham as they took their positions, and Sabine recognized a few of the men, friends of her father's, including Fitzwalter.

And, of course, she was only one of two women.

Seeking out Lady Idalia, Sabine caught the other woman's eye. Idalia was always quick to smile, and she did so now. Sabine had never met a nicer woman. From the day they met nearly a fortnight earlier, they had hardly stopped talking. About their husbands. Their families. The order. Their roles in it. Guy had asked her that morning if she was prepared to part with the other woman.

Indeed, she was not, but the order's plans required it. They fully anticipated John would send forces against them after this day. So they would disperse to two different locations, both of which could withstand a lengthy siege.

Lance and Idalia with Terric in the north. She and Guy with Conrad at Licheford.

For once this oath was taken, they were at war with their king.

"I believe we are ready," Conrad's voice boomed. She could not see him from her vantage point, but Sabine did spy Langton through the crowd. She watched as he made the sign of the cross, the others in this small chapel at Bury St. Edmunds doing the same.

"In nomine Patris et Filii et Spiritus Sancti."

Sabine bowed her head in awe at the sudden and complete silence. When Guy reached for her hand, she gave it to him gladly. The seriousness of this moment suddenly scared her. Of course, she'd known all along what they were doing. The day Noreham's men had come for Guy wrestled in her brain with the memory of learning her parents were never returning home.

But the past two months had also been so full of love and joy. Though they'd not stayed in one place long, Sabine found she didn't mind at all. She was becoming accustomed to the life they would hopefully someday lead when all of this was behind them and Guy had his own mercenary company to command.

When he was finished, Guy released her. And though he did not move his hand to the sword at his side, she knew him well enough to know he was preparing for the worst.

"We gather here today," Conrad boomed, "to pledge an oath upon this altar. The charter that we've altered together, the agreement that we've forged . . ." He paused, and Sabine exchanged a glance with Idalia. "It will be presented to our sovereign. It is the will of all those present for King John to accept the Charter of Liberties, a proclamation of King Henry, here modified by each of us. And if he will not"—she could see Conrad now through a break in the crowd —"we will gain the support we need to remove him as our king."

Somehow, even after all the discussions they'd had over the past weeks, Sabine wasn't prepared for his words.

Every man, and woman, in this room was now an enemy to King John's rule. This day would become a part of history, though Sabine had no idea on which side they would land.

The victors?

Or the defeated?

"Come." Guy pulled her hand once more.

She hadn't heard the rest of Conrad's words, but at Guy's insistence, she followed him toward the front of the chapel. One by one, those ahead of them placed a hand on the altar and repeated the same words.

But Lance, Idalia, Terric, and Conrad had not yet done so.

They stood to the side, as did she and Guy when they finally made their way to the front.

Finally, it was their turn. As one, they placed their hands together upon the altar, with Langton looking on.

Conrad led the recitation and they joined in:

"*Ut suscitem iuramentum est iurare per Deum invoco hodie datum est.*"

So it was done.

And just like before, when they'd entered the chapel, Sabine endured less than friendly glances from some of the men, with the exception of Robert Fitzwalter, who apparently had no qualms about women being involved in this endeavor. His secret smile as he walked by made her heart swell thinking of her father. Sabine caught up with Idalia.

"We need to get them away from here, and swiftly," Lance said.

Idalia looked back to her husband.

"If a blacksmith and a mercenary belong, surely we do as well."

They stood to the side at the front of the chapel as the men filtered out.

"Surely, though I do not believe all who are present agree with you."

Idalia did not appear concerned.

"Some would say 'tis not so coveted, a place at this gathering."

"And others," the Scot replied, sidling up to them, "would say 'tis the most coveted gathering of them all."

Terric Kennaugh, chief of Clan Kennaugh and Earl of Dromsley.

Sabine had met him just the day before. The man was massive. Bigger than all of the others. He did not smile as easily as Guy, though thankfully not as rarely as Lance. Sabine had asked her new friend how she endured her husband's seemingly never-ending frowns.

"That," she'd said in response to Sabine's jest, "is Lance's happy face."

The women had laughed so hard Sabine's stomach hurt.

"Aye, so coveted hardly any remain just moments after taking their oath," Idalia quipped back.

Indeed, everyone had been quick to leave the chapel. Some had already fetched their mounts while others spoke softly to each other. The mood was as somber as the cold, grey day.

Sabine remained silent. She didn't know the clan chief well enough to comment. Instead, she listened to his easy conversation with Idalia, who'd come to know him quite well over the past months. It still shocked her that four such different men had become so close.

They were brothers, and Sabine was grateful Guy had found them. He needed this bond more than the rest, with perhaps Lance as an exception. She knew he'd never truly gotten past his mother's desertion. And his father . . . even Guy had no idea if he was in England or France, though Guy assured her he'd turn up one day, as he always did.

These men, the order, were his family.

And now they were hers.

"So quiet, lady wife."

She hadn't seen him coming.

"Just thinking of . . . things."

"Can we think of things on the way to Licheford?" He shivered, pretending to be cold, although Sabine knew it hardly bothered him. Guy had told her that he was accustomed to all varieties of weather, fair and foul, having campaigned in the outdoors most of his life.

No one cares about the conditions when they secure a mercenary for a mission, he'd said.

"I feel that you have an ulterior motive, husband," she said now.

His smile confirmed that he did indeed.

"We've just committed ourselves," Terric said, "to the most treasonous act imaginable, and you're concerned about bedding your wife." He rolled his eyes. "At least all is normal where Guy is concerned."

Their laughter attracted the others, Lance and Conrad joining their small group as the last of the men dispersed.

"It is done." Lance took Idalia's hand.

"Langton agreed to deliver the missive."

The missive demanding John treat with them.

"You will send me with him?" Guy asked.

Conrad stood closest to the chapel wall. He leaned against it as if he were in no hurry to part ways. "Aye."

The group fell silent. That the archbishop would also be bringing the message to John was a bold statement, to be sure.

"The man has bigger bollocks than you, Guy," Lance said.

Sabine tried hard not to visualize Guy's bollocks just then. And failed. She guessed her cheeks reddened because the laughter only increased, with Sabine swatting Terric on the arm.

"I hope your sister does come to visit. Someone needs to tame this big brute."

Sabine looked at Guy as he explained, "Cait has not been to England, to Dromsley, since . . ."

"We've much to do." Lance pulled Idalia close. "Now that the oath has been taken, we have as much support as we're likely to receive."

"Not all of it." Terric nodded his head toward the north. "My brother is sending men to Dromsley."

"No."

They all said it at the same time.

"This is not your clan's fight," Lance said.

Terric did not appear to agree. "But it is mine. Which makes it theirs too."

The mood had shifted and Sabine wasn't sure why. It was only after the group had finished discussing their plans and parted ways that she was able to ask Guy what had happened back at the chapel.

They rode south, to Licheford. Conrad and two of his men rode ahead of them, far enough that she felt free to speak openly.

"What happened back there? Why does no one want Terric to bring his men to England?"

"'Tis complicated." He slowed and rode closer to her. "What happened that day we met, to Cait . . . he's never forgiven the man who attempted to rape her."

"The one who's dead?" Sabine was not attempting to be flippant, but she found it hard to understand.

"It . . . affected her. Cait loved attending that tournament. Bradon Moor is isolated, their closest neighbors a three-day ride away. After that year, she stopped coming. Has never been to England or Dromsley since. Which is why we were surprised at the possibility she would do so now, especially in the midst of, well, all this."

"I can understand that, but what does it have to do with Clan Kennaugh?"

"Some believe, including Terric's brother Rory, that he should not be involved in our fight. But since that day . . . his hatred for the king's men, even though it was a different king then, runs deep. He sees John's abuse of power as part of a larger problem. That too much power brings out the worst in men. Some don't see the connection—between Cait's attacker and the current king's abuses. But Terric sees it clearly."

"Clearly enough"—she understood now—"to risk men his brother believes should remain in Scotland."

Guy nodded. "Aye."

Sabine whistled, or tried to. She'd never been good at it. "Is Dromsley really the best place for Idalia amidst all of this?"

His look was sympathetic. "We've no notion of where John might lash out first. If he does not agree to meet and decides to make war against his own men, we are all targets. Licheford. Dromsley. Every one of those men who gave their oath back there could see their land or lives taken at any moment."

She knew all of this, but . . .

"Licheford and Dromsley are both well fortified. They are as safe as anywhere."

Despite it, she worried for her new friend. The borderlands were dangerous even without the hostile inner workings of a clan chief at odds with his own people.

Guy had stopped so suddenly, she didn't even realize what he was about until he'd dismounted. Shouting ahead for Conrad to continue, he reached up for her, and just like that, Sabine was in her husband's arms.

Their mounts danced around them, both pairs of reins in Guy's hands.

He kissed her, hard. And Sabine did not hold back.

When he was finished, she gave him a questioning look.

"This talk of treason and death . . . it will consume us if we allow it."

"I just worry for Idalia . . ."

"As I worry for you. But she has Lance, as you have me. On this day and every one after it."

Sabine smiled. "I will not be blackmailed by a nun. Do you remember? 'Tis one of the first things you ever said to me."

Guy laughed. "I remember it well. A beautiful, saucy nun whom I would soon call my wife."

"I had no one. And now, to be a part of this family that is your order—"

"Our order."

"We will get through this together."

Guy kissed the tip of her nose. "Indeed we will, lady wife."

And then he smacked her on the backside, reminding her that it was no civilized gentleman she had married. But she had something better. Her very own mercenary.

LOOK FOR TERRIC'S STORY NEXT IN THE SCOT coming in November 2019.

BECOME AN INSIDER

We may not be knights intent on toppling a monarchy, but the Blood and Brawners are certainly one fun group of romance readers who enjoy being teased (actually, that drives them crazy but I do it anyway) and chatting all things romance reading and hunky heroes.

Facebook.com/Groups/BloodandBrawn

Not on Facebook? Get updates via email by becoming a CM Insider. Delivered bi-weekly, this includes "My Current Obsessions" as well as sneak peeks and exclusive giveaways.

CeceliaMecca.com/Insider

ENJOY THIS BOOK?

Reviews are extremely important for any author and an essential way to spread the word about the Order of the Broken Blade. There is nothing more important that having a committed and loyal group of readers share their opinion with the world.

If you enjoyed this book, I would be extremely grateful if you could leave a short review on the book's Amazon page. You can jump there now by clicking the link below.

Review The Mercenary

The Mercenary: Book 2
The Scot:Book 3 (Coming 2019)
The Earl: Book 4 (Coming 2020)

ABOUT THE AUTHOR

Cecelia Mecca is the author of medieval romance, including the Border Series, and sometimes wishes she could be transported back in time to the days of knights and castles. Although the former English teacher's actual home is in Northeast Pennsylvania where she lives with her husband and two children, her online home can be found at CeceliaMecca.com. She would love to hear from you.

Made in the USA
Las Vegas, NV
05 January 2023